ALL YOUR FAULT

NJ MOSS

For my wife, Krystle
And for my mum, Betsy

1

It was supposed to be sunny when my little sister died. The weather forecast had promised a clear blue sky and a pleasant late-summer evening. But then deep grey clouds had suddenly appeared, and rain slashed down with a vengeance.

Mother and Father had bought Hope a bike for her birthday. Hot pink, it looked like it'd been transported out of a 1950s American catalogue, with tassels on the handlebars and a white wicker basket on the front. Mother had asked me to take her out, since I was thirteen and needed to start adopting some responsibility.

I'd heard them discussing it, Mother with her dignified voice pitched low. "When I was half her age I was self-sufficient, Nick," she said, as I pressed my ear against the dining room door and tried to be as silent as Hope would soon be. "She must learn. They both must. It will be good for Hope to be able to trust her big sister, to feel she can rely upon her if, God forbid, something were to happen to us."

Mother had been raised by a schizophrenic woman who'd taken her own life in one of the most gruesome ways imaginable; she'd slit her throat and then hanged herself for good measure. Mother had seen a glimpse of her dangling body, I knew. And to make matters even more evil, her father had sometimes amused himself by toying with his sick wife's psychosis. He'd created phantoms that weren't there. He'd told her to wake up when she was already awake. He'd punished her for not being the wife he thought he deserved.

I learnt all of this later. But it was this reasoning that led Mother to believe it would be a good idea for me to take care of Hope. We were supposed to bond as sisters. I was supposed to become mature and reliable.

Hope was definitely not supposed to die.

My little sister was like an ambassador for heaven, a perfect girl, her deep oaken hair worn in a long braid down her back, somehow full of vitality even as it drooped in the downpour. She was fond of finding pebbles and small rocks on the beach at Weston-super-Mare, a short drive from Bristol where we lived. She had Father drill holes in them and made necklaces and bracelets and decorations.

She was wearing a small rock-seashell bracelet, her summer dress sticking to her bird-thin body, a body that would have no chance against a speeding bullet of a car. Her dress had little rabbits on it.

Her smile didn't break as we trudged up Clifton Hill. I had no clue that in a matter of minutes she would be lying in a puddle of rain and blood. "It's not too bad." She pushed her bike steadily. "It's kind of nice. It's fun." She raised her voice over the cacophonous rainfall. "Grace, I said it's kind of nice!"

"I heard you." I laughed, shaking my head and sending droplets scurrying. It was difficult to believe how optimistic she was. She didn't even care I'd dragged her halfway across the city so I could see a boy. "I'm pretty fucking miserable though."

She tutted. "Don't curse, Grace."

I held my hands up in defeat. "You sound like Mum."

It was *Mum* then. She had yet to take on the steely *Mother*.

We crested the toughest part of the hill and the rain got worse. But it was only a short way. Soon we'd be warm and safe at home. I had a mobile – a big chunky Nokia – but the battery was dead. Then Hope stopped and turned her bike back toward the direction of the decline.

"Why've you stopped, you little pest?"

"I really think I could." She was moving the bike back and forth as though winding up for something.

"Could what?" I yelled over the rain.

"This hill," she yelled back. "I really think I could, you know. I'm getting good."

"Could *what*?"

"Ride all the way to the bottom. It'd be so fun, wouldn't it?" I could read the adventurous glint in her eyes, the invincible force of her smile. She'd clearly been imagining this for some time.

"We should go home. You can kill yourself another time." What an unfair choice of words; what a horrid memory to have implanted in my mind. "Mum's going to be worried sick."

"I really think I could, Grace. I really do."

"Another time—"

"It won't take long."

"Another time—"

"I can do it."

"Another time. It's raining."

"Don't be a spoilsport."

She moved so fast, the speed of a precocious girl who might've grown up to be a scientist or a champion skier or a fashion designer or anything she wanted. She was brave and never flinched in the face of rain or hills or danger.

She climbed onto the bike and ducked her head and her braid waved behind her, and she crested the lip of the hill and surged back the way we'd come.

I screamed and ran down the hill, tripping and catching myself, panting for breath. Rainwater soaked me and my feet were cold, and then I finally found her, my courageous little sister. Her bike was crumpled like paper and looked tragic in the rain. One wheel was imploded and the other was spinning around and around and around.

2

I felt as if I'd climbed from a memory hole as I stared into the faces of the book club.

There was Yasmin Shenton, a woman with dyed pink hair and a punkish attitude who I'd met through the riding society at Bristol University. Then there was Margaret Basset and Sarah Jenkins, the former a dignified older lady with a dignified bearing and a dignified way of sipping her rosé, the latter a stocky short-haired woman with a penchant for fiddling with her glasses and arguing about politics after a few beers.

It was Mike Foreman, the only man in the group, who leaned forward and nodded slowly. "It's good to draw on your personal experiences."

I exchanged a look with Yasmin, my oldest true friend, though we were both so busy these days that our university closeness was difficult to maintain. It had ridden off with our penchant for horseback riding. Now we were mothers, wives. *Men*, her look said.

Mike was sinewy and wore a baggy black hoodie and faded blue jeans. He had a devilish look in his eyes. I was often surprised he had decided to attend a book club. "It's really helped me connect to the way Esther feels in this scene."

We were discussing Sylvia Plath's *The Bell Jar* – Yasmin's choice – and I'd offered up my final evening with Hope as a talking point, something I found myself doing from time to time, as if by discussing it I could diffuse its messiness.

"Yes, well," I said non-committally, moving my finger around the rim of my wine glass. The pub was dusky with the setting September sun. The bell was yet to be rung for last orders, but already it was quiet, the music playing low, the rain tapping lightly against the window.

It's like Hope is clawing her fingernails against the glass.

There it came again: my unhelpful habit for unhealthy thoughts.

"I really oughtn't to have mentioned it. But I suppose I *can* connect with her character easier than I might like to." I found myself wringing the paperback as though I was punishing it. Matters were not helped by it being the anniversary of Hope's death, my innocent little sister. Mother's face flashed across my mind in a jagged vignette.

"It makes sense," Yasmin said, after a pause.

"Hear hear," Margaret concurred, gesticulating as though she wished she held a gavel.

"Are you okay?" Sarah asked.

"Yes." I laughed, harder than I intended. "I'm sure the last thing you need on a Sunday evening is for me to utterly depress you."

"Don't be stupid." Yasmin shook her head. "You haven't upset anyone."

Except maybe myself. I grabbed my wine glass and knocked it back, finishing off the tiniest of sips, and then turned to Mike. "What did you think anyway?" It was his turn.

He nodded slowly with his characteristic smirk. When he'd

first started, I'd been convinced he was here as a ploy to meet women. But he'd never made a pass at any of us, even tattooed wild-looking Yasmin... and never mind that her surface wildness hid a hard-working accountant and loyal wife and mother. He hadn't known that at the time.

"I think death is a complicated thing, I guess." Mike shrugged. "I think it's hard to know if we've done the right thing, in life or in death, you know?" He chuckled. "I also think I'd like another bloody pint before things get too serious."

"Sounds perfect," Sarah said. "Cider and black?"

"You read my mind."

Yasmin reached across the table and took my hand, giving it a squeeze. I met her eyes and we both smiled. I remembered eleven years ago, how tall and majestic we were on horseback. It seemed like a *hundred* years ago, a thousand. I felt like a different woman. I was a different woman.

"Are you having another, Grace?" Sarah asked me.

"No. I'm driving. Thank you."

Had Hope's killer been drunk the evening he ran her down? I'd never know.

He'd hit, and then he'd run. Even calling the killer *he* was pure sexism on my part. The killer was a shadow, a faceless driver, a lost car slicing through our lives and leaving cataclysm in its wake.

3

I drove from the pub in the city centre toward Filton, to our three-bedroom semi we were just about holding on to. With Troy's job as a manager at an insurance company, along with my occasional sprees of part-time work – receptionist, office temp, retail work, things Mother would always tip her nose up at, as though *her* daughter was above such things – we were managing to balance the difficult juggling act of modern life.

I was eager for this day to be over, for Hope's death to be another year behind me. Even if it was cruel – and it was cruel – I longed for the day when I could forget it completely. It haunted me. The guilt gnawed. I knew the chances of me overcoming the grief were slim, and if I thought overly long about it I might go the same way as Cecilia Hyde, my grandmother.

I shook my head, squeezing the steering wheel, telling myself I was being foolish. I was not, nor had I ever been, what could be characterised as mad. Nor would I become so. At thirty, I had passed the threshold for the risk of schizophrenia. It was most likely to strike in your twenties or late teens.

What about Mia? What about Russ?

I went inside and found Troy in the living room, sitting in his writer's cubby. A *Lord of the Rings* poster hung on the wall above his desk and a few action figures – no, *collectibles* – stood sentinel around his laptop. As my husband spun in the office chair and smiled up at me, I saw the gaunt man he'd been at university, as though he could survive on passion alone. He'd had an almost rakish appearance then. Now, just as I had, he'd filled into his body, a few lines around his eyes that hinted at what would come in another decade.

I felt a wave of love crash over me, so glad to be home. I slid into his lap and wrapped my arms around his shoulders.

"Woah." He laughed. "What's this for?"

"What?" I wriggled against him, feeling his desire flame. "I can't be happy to see my husband? Are the children in bed?"

Troy smiled, his goatee shifting with his lips, stroking his hand up and down my thigh. "Just about. Russ was really good tonight, built a bridge out of Lego. I swear to God, Grace, the kid's gonna be an architect when he grows up."

A glow infused me, even as the elephant in the room tried to stampede over the moment. I could see the Word document open on Troy's laptop; the word count was only one hundred more than when I'd left. I knew it was several hundred shy of his goal for the night.

"How did it go this evening?" I asked.

"It's getting there."

Troy had had a few short stories published in online magazines, but his big dream was to get a novel published set in his fantasy world, the same world all his stories were set in. His Twitter bio advertised this fact. He often said all he needed was a chance, one shot, and he'd shock the world.

"I know it's going to be amazing." I kissed his bristly-bearded mouth. "Just like you."

"Somebody's feeling frisky tonight."

"Frisky?" I giggled. "I was about to offer you-know-what, but now I think I may be sick instead." He made to tickle me and I leapt up, a pre-emptive defence. "I'm going to check on the little ones. Then maybe..."

He jumped to his feet and leaned forward, kissing me harder. "Forget *maybe*. See you in three. I'll put on my best lingerie. I'm feeling *frisky*."

"I'm not listening." I laughed as I strode from the room.

I went upstairs and poked my head into Russ's room. My son was shrouded in his blanket, curled on his side with a content smile on his face. The only time he wasn't moving was when he was sleeping. I walked across the room and kissed him on the forehead. "I love you, little man."

I went into Mia's room. While Russ's was a war zone of Legos and toys and five-year-old detritus – despite our efforts to the contrary – Mia's was a little lady's boudoir. Her art supplies sat neatly on her desk, and her walls were decorated with all the drawings and paintings she'd done since she was three, the quality changing from crude stickmen to stunningly precise pencil sketches and flourishes of vivid paint that held personality in each brushstroke. She had real talent. Pride swelled in me every time I looked at her work.

There was only one that didn't fit: a big A3-sized piece of a woman sitting in the middle of what appeared to be a collapsing star, her dress torn and tattered, but thankfully covering her private areas. Everything about it hinted at a terrorised spirit, which was fitting; it had belonged to my grandmother. Mother had given it as a gift, and I'd felt awkward telling her no.

Mia had her back to me, snoring softly. For the briefest moment as I gazed across the room, illumed only by the lamp posts and the moonlight against the curtains, I saw Hope. Hope at ten years old, three older than she'd ever be. Sleeping peacefully.

My phone buzzed as I walked down the hall toward our

bedroom.

It was an email from a company called Langdale Consulting. I'd set up a LinkedIn profile a few weeks ago in anticipation for Russ starting school. I'd felt faintly ridiculous filling in my two years of university and my patchy work experience. But I needed to at least try.

The terse email informed me they were interested in interviewing me for the position of personal assistant to Clive Langdale, the CEO. I clicked the link. I had to check the yearly pro-rata salary twice, and then again – and one more time to be prudent – before I allowed myself to believe it. It was almost double what I'd expected to be making. Plus it was part-time, meaning I could work around the children.

The interview was for tomorrow. Russ's first day of school.

Troy walked into the room, laptop under his arm. "All good?"

I told him about the job, the interview, the opportunity. His face lit up when I mentioned the salary. "I can't believe they'd consider me. The pay is so high for the position. They must want somebody with experience, surely. Maybe there was a mix-up."

"Work isn't all about the CV." He sat on the bed beside me. "They must see how special you are." I rolled my eyes. "I mean it. You're passionate. You're hard-working. Look at how you're raising those kids. You're amazing, and maybe they can see that."

I felt my cheeks redden in the special way only Troy could achieve, even after a decade of marriage. "So you think I should go for it?"

"What harm can it do?"

He was right. And we needed the money. Neither of us would say it, but Troy was having problems at work. Every week it was another catastrophe. This could save us, save our family, make it so we could enjoy our lives instead of fret all the time.

I clicked Reply.

4

Rolling out of bed early the next morning, I felt my anxiety doing a twisty dance through my body. Not only was I interviewing for the absolute perfect job today – not my dream job, per-se, but the job that would best support my family – it was also Russ's first day at big school.

I peeled the curtains back slightly, peering into the garden. I looked at Russ's swing and his little football goal. My chest got tight as I stared at the sun-flecked flower beds, thinking about how soon it'd grow cold and grey.

I remembered these past five years, how I'd felt fused to my son. Even after he'd started preschool, he'd only done half days. The afternoons had been ours. Our world had consisted of private beautiful adventures. There was a simple happiness in sitting in the park and watching my son stampede around, sometimes playing with his friends if the other daytime parents joined us, otherwise content to amuse himself for hours on end.

I felt that era of my life fading, a new one beginning. The selfish part of me screamed to stop it. *Stop it.* Grab Russ and take him to the library, sit him down in front of his favourite monster-truck book and wander the aisles myself, or perhaps pack a picnic and abscond for the day, build estates out of wet sand.

I wanted him to start school, of course. I wanted him to succeed. But I was losing my best friend.

I sorted through my wardrobe, searching for the clothes I'd change into when I returned from the school run. The interview was not until the afternoon so there was no use going there directly after dropping them off. I stared at the heeled shoes, the pencil skirt, the tights, the white shirt, the snug blazer. I tried to envision myself wearing them, a working woman, a modern woman. I found it far more difficult than I thought I would.

"Grace?" Troy yawned. "What time is it?"

"Early."

"Can't sleep?"

"I'm a little nervous."

"You'll be fine." He was already half-asleep again. "I know you will. And don't worry about Russ. He's a little soldier. He's going to do great today."

He rolled over and buried his head in his pillows, a habit he'd cultivated since his work problems had started. I could tell he wished he could stay sleeping, living in his dreams, pretending work didn't exist.

If I got this job, that might change. He might have the freedom to find something new. I tried not to let the pressure niggle. But there was no denying it. Today mattered a lot.

5

"Mummy, do you think I can have a bajillion new school friends?" Russ beamed from his booster seat, which he hated sitting in. Of course, *he* was old enough for a big-boy seat. But cars were dangerous, deadly things, and I wasn't taking any chances. My youngest was always a ball of barely contained energy, and this morning was no different. He was tall and sturdy for his age, with his father's curly brown hair and his grandfather's – my father's – pale green eyes. "Or one really, really amazing one?"

I smiled at him in the rear-view mirror, a film of sweat coating my body. I wished I could be as optimistic as him, but I felt like a bird about to release her fledgling into the open air, which was good, necessary, but it was also terrifying. There were predators in the sky.

What if he didn't like it? What if he wanted to come home?

My mind whirred and a maelstrom of uncertainty spun and spun, like the bike wheel, Hope's bicycle wheel, had spun around and around and—

"Mummy? The light."

"Oh," I said, just in time for an impatient driver two cars down to give me the mother of all honks. "Silly Mummy."

"You're not silly, Mummy."

"No? Then what am I?"

"Umm." He tapped his chin, a gesture he'd adopted after seeing Troy do it the previous month. "You're funny. Funny Mummy."

I smiled and followed the flow of traffic, smelling the last moments of summer through the window. Mia had her blood-red headphones in, her pencil making quiet *tsk* noises as she sketched.

"Mia, how many friends have you got?" Russ asked, tugging at the headphones.

"Russie. Play nice."

Mia and I met eyes in the rear-view mirror. She gave a shrug that was somehow grown-up. She was only ten and yet sometimes I saw her as the young woman she would all too soon become, my little miracle Mia, the answer who had come midway through my university career. I'd never resented dropping out and giving birth to her instead of finishing my psychology studies. I was quite amazed by that.

"Pardon?" she said patiently, turning to Russ.

"I said how many friends do you got."

"Do you *have*. Um, I don't know. A few. Who cares?"

"I want loads. I've got Jack and Nathan and they're in my class but I want loads and *loads*."

"I don't care. There's more to life than being popular."

How was she only ten, this precocious girl, so like Hope, so mature for her age? I knew she'd set the world ablaze one day and leave us all dazzled in the light. People would gawp in amazement when I told them I was Mia Hope Dixon's mother. *The famous artist?* they'd gasp.

"Mummy," Russ went on, as we inched through Bristol

Monday-morning traffic. "Are you dressing that to your intervoo?"

"Wearing," Mia said. "Interview."

"Absolutely." I waved a hand down at my hoodie and jogging bottoms and my UGG boots. "Because then I won't get the job and I can spend all day with you."

"Nah-uh," he said, breaking my heart a little. "I'm a *schoolboy*."

He looked so smart in his uniform, the burgundy sweatshirt and the pleated black trousers, his shiny polished shoes. Did all mothers feel this way when their children started school, properly started it, the nine-to-three robbery?

Yasmin had cracked a bottle of champagne when her oldest began Reception. "I'm free. No longer shall I be a Victorian handmaiden to an attention-hungry brat." I'd laughed along with her.

And of course part of me was ready to reclaim my days. But there was this ache too, as though somebody was stealing him away. "Co-dependency is not a flattering trait in a mother," my mother had told me once after a few glasses of wine. "We are here to enable our children to function independently in the world, not to hold their hands through every tiny incident."

Fine. I get it. But maybe I love my son and maybe I'm sad and maybe I don't want to drink champagne. Fuck you all.

I'd been through this with Mia, but I'd had Russ to focus on. With him gone I had to be a proper person again. For the first time in my life I was praying for gridlocked traffic.

There was no such luck. The traffic eased and on we drove.

Soon I was parked up outside the school gates and Mia was taking her headphones out and folding everything into her rucksack, which had a little van Gogh pin on the strap. "You're going to do great today, Mum."

Russ fidgeted, buzzing to be out and gone.

We climbed from the car. Mia waited beside her little brother, ready to walk him in as we'd discussed. It meant a lot to her, I knew, helping him. It was good for them to be able to rely on each other, of course. It was nothing like me and Hope.

There were embarrassed tears in my eyes as I leaned down and wrapped my arms around my son. "I love you."

"Love you, Mummy," he said gleefully. "Bye-bye."

I watched them walk off together, Russ romping, ready. I wiped at my face and coughed back a sob, knowing it was silly. There were far, far bigger problems in the world. It was self-indulgent. Mother would grimace if she could see me now. *Are you under the impression they're off to a labour camp, dear?*

I climbed into the car and blinked and felt the hot tears sliding down my cheeks. There was a little voice inside of me – it was always there – telling me I didn't deserve any of this. I was too rotten and broken. I ignored it, like I always did. I was very good at sequestering that voice. It was Mother. It was self-doubt and anxiety and hatred and all the bad things in life. It was an itch that, if scratched, could destroy everything Troy and I had built. It was useless and I wished it would die, this voice, this whisper.

The only thing you deserve is a blade to the throat and a rope around your neck.

But that wasn't true.

And I was allowed to cry if I felt like crying.

6

I was all twitching energy as I drove to the waterfront, near
Queen's Square, where Langdale Consulting was located.
My clothes were clinging far too stickily to me, my tights
gripping like nylon hands. I wanted to unbutton my shirt, but it
would hardly make a good impression to walk into the interview
with my bra hanging out. Or maybe it would? Maybe if I had a
lascivious wink ready to go, a little suggestive head tilt, it might
work in my favour. *Do they have casting couches in the management
consulting industry?* I laughed inwardly. *If so, Mr Langdale, I'd very
much like to see it, if you please.*

After searching for twenty minutes, I found a parking space
about a half-mile from the offices. I walked through Queen's
Square, the sun shining. A young couple strolled by, glued to
each other in their intimacy, and for a moment I remembered
walking hand-in-hand with Troy through this same park, about
their age.

We'd had the whole world ahead of us. Maybe we still did.

I found a café nearby – I was woefully early – and ordered an
apple juice, since caffeine was a no-no for me. I'd kicked the
stuff when I was pregnant with Russ, and this time, unlike with

Mia, it had stuck. I'd always had problems with caffeine. Heart palpitations, anxiety, excessive sweating. Now, without my body having any tolerance, an occasional coffee felt like a line of Class-A drugs.

The buildings around here were redbrick and stylish, hipster-chic, the sort of place I could imagine Yasmin feeling right at home. I felt like a frumpy mum at a rave. I watched the café window as dyed heads and shaved heads and beanie hats bobbed by, and I tried to take deep breaths and calm myself.

Getting this job would mean a lot to our family.

We were not on the cusp of disaster, fine, but neither was disaster a far-off notion. All it would take was one minor tragedy, one expense we had not foreseen, and then our month-to-month existence would come toppling down.

Asking my parents for money was out of the question. It was worse than that. It was a death of sorts. The death of the person I was meant to have become after Hope died. After that rainy blood-soaked evening, once the dust had settled – if it ever had – I understood I'd need to fulfil the role of two daughters. I'd have to achieve, excel, transcend. I would be what Hope would've been.

I'd already failed once by dropping out of university. To go to them with hat in hand would be the final blow. I'd taken their favourite daughter. I should have protected her. It was my fault. All of this was unsaid. We did not discuss matters like this openly in my family. But it was there, lurking like an alligator beneath the surface, ready to snap its ugly teeth.

Troy's parents were just as complicated. His father was a by-the-bootstraps type, a man who believed hard work would conquer all. He'd gone from a council estate to an upmarket detached four-bedroom house through sheer force of will, working eighteen-hour days to create a successful home removals company. I knew Troy would detest going to him. His brother, Keith, was a successful photographer working in America, and this was all the ammunition George Dixon could wish for. "See," he'd said one Christmas, proudly displaying a magazine with one of Keith's nature photographs on the cover. "Hard work, son, hard work pays off."

The implication was that any financial failure, under any circumstances, was for lack of hard work. How could he think any different? He'd slept three hours a night for years while building up his business. What was Troy doing in his spare time? How was his book coming along? Was he putting in the blood, the grit, the sweat, the tears?

I picked up my apple juice and took a small sip, checking the time. I had an hour. It seemed far too long to sit here thinking.

7

Clive Langdale's office wall was dominated by a canvas of a snowy mountain, sunlight shining over the peak, with a motivational quote scrawled across the bottom. *You Miss Every Shot You Don't Take.* The photo and the words seemed mismatched to me, but I was hardly about to point that out as I sat there, wringing my hands, staring at his empty office chair.

His chair, I noticed, was twice as large as mine. It was a throne.

I had been led to his office by a woman called Olivia Melhuish. I was almost certain I'd detected some resentment in the way she'd spoken to me, but perhaps that was my overactive mind. God knew the women in our family had some self-sabotaging instincts.

My grandmother had slit her throat and then hanged herself. It was simple common sense. Why take the risk of surviving?

Relax, Grace.

Finally, the door opened and I sprung to my feet like an overeager kid. *Pick me, pick me.*

I turned to find a shiny-toothed man with a receding hairline and a Rolex glinting at his wrist. His suit was steel-coloured and his stride was brisk. He looked at his desk and at the sofa area off to the side, and then nodded shortly.

"No need for all the ceremony." He walked over to the armchair and sat down, folding one leg over the other.

I followed him. "Of course."

The word *unorthodox* was already bouncing around my mind. On the way in, I'd passed a games room with a pool table, as well as a small workout room. Several of the employees were tattooed and had dyed hair. I supposed I'd had some old-fashioned notions of office work from never having properly participated in it. Or perhaps my experience in temp work had been at old-school companies. This company screamed – or wanted to scream – modern.

I sat and folded my hands, wishing my throat was not so dry. I didn't want to ask for water. I glanced at the door.

"No, Mrs Dixon, it's just us."

"Please, call me Grace."

"Then I'm Clive." He smiled in a corporate sort of way. I wondered if he was secretly laughing at me. *Paranoid. Calm down.* "Okay, well, let me be blunt. I don't give a damn about any of the human resources shit I'm supposed to ask you. I've got this big list of questions but where's the fun in that? No, *hell* no. If you're going to be my personal assistant, I need to do this my way."

"Sure," I said, waiting.

"So tell me why, Grace."

"Why?"

"Why do you want this job?"

What a broad question. I searched my mind. I'd read a "Ten Tips to Ace Your Interview" article online the previous night, sitting up in bed, sex-sore and contented beside Troy. At no point had they mentioned this approach.

Because I need the money. Why do you think, Clive?

"I want a challenge. I've been out of the work force for quite a few years."

I winced. It sounded so cut-and-paste. Plus I'd reminded him of my inexperience.

"Why did you leave your last position?"

I fought the urge to pick at the sofa, stab at it with my fingernails to give my hands something to do. "Scheduling issues. My son was still in preschool and they weren't exactly flexible about my working hours."

I silently pleaded for him not to ask why I hadn't enrolled him in afternoon preschool, because then I'd have to admit I'd greedily kept my son for myself. I'd let my emotions guide me. It didn't look good, as though I was some tragic mother hen whose only sense of identity came from her children. I wasn't that, was I? Or if I was, was that really so bad?

"Hmm," he said, thankfully letting my explanation pass. "But *why*?"

I almost groaned. This screamed pretentious. And yet the pay was good. I needed this job. It was perfect.

"My children." I met his eyes. "If you want the truth, Clive – and as your PA, I will always be honest with you – I am here for my children. I want them to be able to look up to me as more than their mother. I want them to be able to look up to me as a strong capable person. Not that there's anything wrong with being a mother. I didn't mean that."

My words didn't sound as crisp as I needed them to be.

"Hmm," he said again. "I suppose that makes sense."

"Do you have children?" I wished I could whip the question back the moment I'd uttered it. It was way too forward.

He did not look pleased. "In a way. But no, not really."

In a way? What in the name of Christ was that supposed to mean?

"My girlfriend has a daughter." Perhaps he could read my confusion. "But I fail to see how it's relevant, sweetheart."

Sweetheart. That really grated. "Of course."

A pause.

The pause was getting longer.

This pause was far, far too lengthy.

"I'll work harder than any other candidate," I said quickly, trying to salvage. My palms were streaming rivers of sweat. "I'm not working for a pay cheque." *Liar.* "Or to 'make ends meet'." *Oh, you lying bitch.* "I'm working for the respect of my children, who I love more than anything in this world. I'll admit I'm surprised, Mr—Clive. I did not expect things to be so informal today. But I'm also glad, because it means I get to tell you a blunt truth. Hire me and I'll work ten times as fucking hard as anybody else you interview. Because I want it more. Plain and simple."

My heart thumped in the back of my throat.

I was fairly certain I'd said the F-word.

Clive nodded slowly and a smile smeared across his face. Unless I was going mad – *maybe you are* – I was sure I detected pity in his expression. "You're right. This is informal. I know you weren't expecting this. Well, we'll be in touch."

"That's... it?"

"I've heard everything I need to hear. Since you're the last candidate I've interviewed, I should have an answer for you within the hour. Please keep your mobile turned on."

"Sure. Yes. Of course. And Clive, I didn't mean to curse. I suppose I got carried away."

He chuckled as he stood up, offering me his hand. His Rolex jingle-jangled as we shook. Thankfully he didn't mention how badly I was sweating. "Nothing wrong with a bit of passion. We could use it around here. Like I said, keep your mobile on."

I left the offices, finding it difficult to look anywhere but at the floor. I rode the lift with a pit in my belly. Barely twenty minutes had passed since I'd entered the building, but it had felt like a saga.

It was over and I'd ruined it. He'd set me some obscure test and I'd been unable to think on my feet quickly enough to dance to his tune.

I wandered Queen's Square for several minutes, clutching my mobile and waiting for the vibration that would tell me, unfortunately – and though I performed very well and I was a very likeable person – I was not quite right for this position.

I kept walking, around and around and around.

Like the wheel of a bicycle. Like the rain-streaked spokes of a novelty pink bike, a 1950s-style bike, with tassels, going around and around—

How is that helpful? I chided myself. Torturous thoughts were the last thing I needed.

I sat on a bench and took long deep breaths, trying to get myself under control. Half an hour passed, sitting there, waiting.

I decided the suddenness of the experience was causing this ribcage-thumping heartbeat. I spent my days doing chores and taking care of Russ. And then, all at once, I was in an office pretending to be like them, pretending my skirt wasn't clingy and my armpits weren't damp. Then there had been the strange informality of the interview. That hadn't helped.

My mobile rang. It was Langdale Consulting.

"Grace." Clive sounded sombre, a man who didn't want to be making this call. I braced for rejection. But then he said, "I won't keep you in suspense. You got the job. You were by far the best candidate."

"Pardon?" I gasped. "Really?"

"Really. I know your circumstances, and I could tell you were nervous back there. But there's no need. The job's yours, if you'll have it. And let me just say, it's never smart to look a gift horse in the mouth."

"No. I mean, yes. Thank you. I agree."

"Come in on Friday for a tour and to meet the gang. We'll get you started properly on Monday. I hope you can hit the ground running."

"Yes, thank you."

"See you soon."

"Goodbye."

He hung up and I felt all the tension deflating out of me. I let my head fall back. I closed my eyes, the sunlight glowing against my eyelids. I'd done it. I'd actually bloody done it.

8

I sat outside the school gates waiting for the bell to ring, the butterflies in my belly taking on a different quality. These were not the razor-winged butterflies of a person unsure of whether or not they were fit to be seen as more than a parent. These were the blissfully regular – but no less special – butterflies of a mother waiting to hear how her son's first day at school went.

I couldn't help but smile, despite the nerves I felt for Russ. In most unusual circumstances, in a most unconventional situation, I'd proven I still had some of my old grit left.

I sat back and closed my eyes, thinking back to the interview, wondering if I'd perhaps exaggerated how poorly it had gone in my mind. Sitting in Queen's Square, had I worked myself into an unnecessary panic?

Memory had been my chief interest while studying psychology at university. I remembered reading the work of a psychologist, whose name I'd forgotten. They'd studied satanic cults and explained how many of the stories had in fact been entirely fictional, despite the tellers firmly believing in them. The study had often returned to me over the years, perhaps because the so-called memories had been so vivid, so full of detail – scents and sounds and visceral violence – and yet they'd sprouted from the emptiness of the mind. In a sense, they were fake. And yet in another sense, they were as real as any other memory, because they *felt* real.

Perhaps we treated our memories like our faces before a night out. A little touch of foundation here, some blusher there, and why not some lipstick, why not some shaper, why not add some contours? What was real when you got right down to it? Our minds were all that existed.

These subjects had once kept me at the library for long nights, consuming textbooks and journal articles like oxygen.

It was entirely possible I'd retroactively made the interview seem worse in my mind, perhaps to soften the blow when the rejection came. The café too, sitting in the café and seeing nothing but hipsters and stylish women... was I projecting, seeing the opposite of myself, because I'd felt mumsy and frumpy? I felt an ember of my old passion, letting my mind skim over these ideas.

Perhaps if I understood memory well enough, I could alter mine, make it so my sister had never turned her bike to the lip of that hill. Or I could forget Father's severe face when he told me the fate of my grandmother and how my mother had led a hard life: how she'd seen Cecilia Hyde swing back and forth in her studio, her throat paint-red.

I groaned, the noise seeming loud in the closeness of the car.

This was a good day and, as I did far too often, I was allowing the more macabre parts of myself to drag my mood into the dirty depressing gutter.

I climbed from the car and sucked in a lungful of fresh air, taking out my mobile as I wandered over to the gates.

I'm so proud of you, Troy's text read. *I knew you could do it. I'll pick us up a Chinese and some bubbly on the way home. You are AMAZING. I love you so much xxx*

I love you, I wrote back. *Picking up the terrors. Hope Russ is okay. See you later xxx*

The bell rang and soon I was milling amongst the other parents. I felt another expansion of pride when a couple of them, ladies I knew by face and first name alone, commented on what I was wearing.

I was grinning like a fool when Russ came sulking out, his teacher, Miss Mathieson, standing at his side with a pained expression on her face.

She was only twenty-six and extremely beautiful, her hair a close-cropped afro and her eyes wide and sharp. She'd published poetry in small local magazines and she ran a creative writing class after school. She was one of those teachers who honestly cared about her charges.

Her frown deepened when she spotted me and came walking over. But worse, Russie wasn't looking at me. He was staring at the ground in a way I recognised well. His hand made a tight fist on the strap of his Iron Man schoolbag.

What's happened? What has he done?

"Mrs Dixon." She kept her voice low, probably aware of how far-reaching the schoolyard grapevine could be. "Can I have a word? In private?"

"Of course, yes." My mouth was dry as I stared at my son and wondered why he wouldn't look at me. "Let me just find my daughter."

9

Mia kept Russ company as Naomi Mathieson and I settled into the classroom. She sat behind her desk and I sat opposite, folding my legs, interlocking my hands in my lap. I was doing everything I could not to fidget. Behind Naomi's head a colourful alphabet hung, the pink *F* upside down where it had come loose from its fastening.

"What's the problem?" I asked.

"There isn't a problem, really, not like this huge *boom*. I want to nip something in the bud before it becomes a problem."

I stared and she stared and I realised she was waiting for me to speak. "Nip what in the bud?"

"Russ, is he... would you say he's quite an energetic boy?"

"Of course he is." My hackles flared. *Leave my son alone, Naomi.* "He's got bundles of energy. It's one of the things that makes him so special."

"And it's great. I don't want you to think it's not. But the problem is—sorry, not problem. What I'd like to *discuss* is that quite a few times today he's disrupted the class. Don't get me wrong. This is Reception. It's expected. But I wanted to see if you could maybe talk to him? Let him know school time is different from playtime?"

"It's his first day." My voice had become like Mother's, as it often did when I felt threatened. It became more cutting. It became *posher*. "I'm certain expecting a boy like Russ, a boy full of energy and life, to instantly adjust to sitting in a classroom all day seems rather ridiculous. Doesn't it?"

Naomi stared at me, face hard. "I'm sorry if you feel like I'm attacking you, Mrs Dixon. That's not what I want to do here."

"What did he do?"

"He jumped up on the tables several times, even after I told him not to. At one point he tried to run out of the class. A flock of birds was passing by the window and he leapt up and ran over, shouting for everybody to look at the birds. Obviously I could handle this myself. But I wanted to speak to you first. It'd be such a shame – for him, for you, for everyone – to start his school career by telling him off. Like you said, he's a ball of energy and that's great. I don't want to stifle him. I'd like to point his energy in the right direction."

She broke off, placing her multi-coloured fingernails on the desk. I knew she was right. She was a good teacher. And yet, at the same time, the urge to slap her across the face swelled in me. What did she expect, a well-trained dog sitting when she said *sit*, standing when she snapped her fingers?

"I understand where you're coming from, Miss Mathieson."

"Please, call me—"

"But like I said before, it's his first day. Of course his behaviour is not acceptable, and I'll talk to him. But I believe some patience is required too. It's completely healthy and natural for a boy his age to have energy to spare. Unless he's in trouble, I would very much like to take him home."

"That's what I'm trying to avoid, Mrs Dixon. Trouble."

"Like I said, I'll speak to him about his behaviour. I'm sure things will go more smoothly tomorrow."

I fled the room and found Mia and Russ in the hallway, Mia scrolling through music on her iPod, Russ sitting with his arms folded, his lips stuck out. He was looking at the floor and trying not to cry. He hated crying. He thought it made him a baby.

Was I too soft with him? Should I scold him now, turn cold and slightly cruel as my mother would have?

"Mummy," he said, looking up at me. "I'm sorry. I'm really, really sorry."

I found myself standing over him, hugging him to my hips, and then kneeling down and wiping a tear from his cheek. "Don't be silly. You're not in trouble. We were having a grown-up talk, that's all."

"Really?"

I smiled. "Really."

"You got the job," Mia said, narrowing her eyes at me.

"How did you know?"

"You look different. You look happy. I'm proud of you."

"Me too!" Russ beamed. "You're the bestest Mummy in the whole wide world!"

I opened my arms and they both fell into the embrace, though Mia half-hugged me, reluctantly. From the classroom, Naomi Mathieson peered at me and smiled tightly. I smiled back, uneasy, secretly wondering if I'd done what was best for my children or what was best for me.

"Come on." I stood and took Russ's hand. Mia drifted away; this was too much for her. "We're having a Chinese tonight."

"With the nice chips?"

"Yes, Russie. With the nice chips."

"Can you tell Dad I want those noodles, Mum?" Mia said. "The ones I had on his birthday?"

I took out my phone, shooting her a wink. "Texting him now, Miss Fussy."

Mia smirked.

10

—————

"I'm telling you, she has it out for me." Troy sighed, his anxiety heavy even through the phone. "I don't understand. I haven't done anything wrong. I do my job. She used to accept that, appreciate it, even. I'm a good manager. I'm fair but stern when I have to be. It's not like this is my fucking dream job, fine. But who works their dream job? Jesus, Grace, lately it's like she has a vendetta against me. Today I submitted this report. It's a run-of-the-mill thing, we submit them every week. It's *basic*."

I nodded along, like I always did, even over the phone. When Troy needed to vent about work, it was best to let him get it all out.

"But she decides to charge into my office and tear me a new one, loudly, so all the agents on the floor hear her shouting at me. How the fuck are they supposed to respect their manager if the Head of Claims can come in here and start chewing my goddamn ear off like some feral dog? It's completely out of order."

I was standing in the garden, leaning against the cool brick of our home, watching as the sky bruised purple. Inside, I could hear Russ at the kitchen table, making ooh and ahh noises as he

34

played Minecraft on the iPad. I was giving him more screen time this evening, which was probably a mistake, most definitely an error in motherhood after he'd misbehaved at school.

But I was tired, my nerves unspooling after the interview and the confrontation with Russ's teacher. I wanted to be the perfect mother, never waning in my efforts to monitor screen time. But when Troy was almost two hours late and Russ was bouncing off the walls and I wanted a stiff drink and a lie down, it was hard.

Troy wasn't done. "And then it's, 'You need to stay late and complete these reports.' I ask her if this is paid overtime or if I'm here for the fun of it, and she looks at me like I'm dirt, like I'm Oliver Fucking Twist begging for a handout. It's driving me insane."

"I know." I felt deflated. "She sounds like she's being very unreasonable."

"Exactly!" he erupted. "That's exactly what she is. Unreasonable. Anyway, look, I'm on my way home. Mia wanted fish and chips, right?"

Our local Chinese doubled as a chippy, but I couldn't remember a time when Mia had ordered the fish. "No. The Korean Udon noodles, the ones she had on your birthday."

"Yeah, that's right. Listen, I'm driving. I've got to go."

"Are you on the Bluetooth?"

The way he sighed truly niggled at me. It was a sigh that told me I was being paranoid. I shouldn't worry about such unimportant things. As though driving safety was unimportant. As though there weren't thirty thousand hit-and-runs every year.

But Troy wouldn't be a runner, a voice whispered inside my head. *He'd do the right thing.*

"You know I wouldn't risk that. I love you. See you soon."

"Love you," I said, but he'd already hung up.

It wasn't that I resented being the sounding board for Troy's work-related ranting. He needed somebody. Of course he did. I was his wife, the perfect candidate. But sometimes it felt like I was being drained of all my positive emotions.

Fine, perhaps there was a desire in me to ignore his work and pretend the Troy we knew was the only one who mattered. Fine, maybe I wished he'd let his troubles with Vicky, his boss, fall to the wayside this evening in light of my good news. Was that selfish? I didn't know. Marriage was difficult sometimes.

I went inside and walked up behind Russ. He was sitting at the kitchen table, pawing at the iPad. "Five more minutes," I told him.

"Ten, please? Can we do ten?"

"Five."

"Five and a half."

I laughed and leaned against the table. "Okay, clever cogs, five and a half it is. What are you doing anyway?"

"Gotta get a thing for my horse. A what's-it-called, Mummy?"

"A saddle?"

"Yeah. Then I can ride it."

"Russie, did you like school today?" I asked as casually as I could. I wanted him to stay focused on the game. "Was it as fun as you'd hoped it would be?"

"No. It was boring. Really really boring. We just sat there and talked and talked and I wanted to go outside, Mummy, because there was a bajillion birds out there. At the park when we run at the birds and they all fly, they fly like little paper airplanes and that's so cool. But then the nasty teacher says *sit down* and everybody was looking at me and it's really horrible."

"What about Jack and Nathan? Did you get to talk to them, hmm?"

He nodded sulkily. Jack and Nathan were his best preschool friends, and were also in his Reception class. "Yeah."

"And what about sitting down? Were you sitting down *all* day?"

36

"Well, no. But it's stand when she says and sit when she told and maybe I want to stretch my legs because that's what you say, Mummy, you say let's *stretch our legs* and do you remember when I used to think that meant we had to make our legs go all like spaghetti when I was really little?"

"Yes, I remember." An ocean flowed beneath my words, trying to shatter my resolve.

"Can we talk to the Miss and you can say I need to come with you in the lunchtimes, and in the mornings I can go there, but then we can do the fun stuff, Mummy? I'll be super quiet and good even when you're in New Look, I promise."

I cursed myself. I should've made him do more than half days at preschool. "Russ, look at me."

"But the horse, Mummy." Despite his outpouring of words, his eyes had remained fused to the iPad.

"Young man."

He looked up at me with Father's pale green eyes. "Mmm?"

"I want you to behave at school." I was as stern as I could muster. "Do you know what I mean when I say behave?"

"No."

"I think you do. Why don't you try to tell me?"

"I should just not have any fun and just sit there and hear the teacher and do what she says. I hate school."

His voice caught. I fought the instinct to embrace him.

"You can still have fun. I'm sure there are lots of activities where you can enjoy yourself. There's playtime. You'll make more friends. But no, I'm sorry, you can't have fun *all* the time."

"Can I play Minecraft now?"

"Did you hear what I said?"

"Yes."

I nodded and gave into the urge, reaching over and rubbing him on the shoulder. "Then yes, you can play Minecraft."

11

Clive dashed around the office as though he was determined to always be several steps ahead of me, striding in his steel-coloured suit, balding head held high. He pointed around the office, talking too quickly for me to keep up. I clipped along next to him in my heels and my business attire, trying to project the image of a woman who knew what she was doing.

"And this is finance, but I doubt you'll have much to do with them. They're pretty self-sufficient. Don't do anything stupid like spunk the expenses at a strip club and you'll be golden. Joking. Here's Zora, the office gossip. Joking."

Please tell me you're joking one more time.

My head was spinning, but I made myself seem at ease – or tried to – as we stood over the desk. Zora had dyed silver hair cropped close to her head. Her forearm sported a tattoo, some sort of Viking-style thing, like a hieroglyph or a rune, and when she looked up at me, there was a knowing glint in her pale Nordic eyes.

"Oh, and you are Grace," she said with a Scandinavian accent.

"Yes." I was suddenly overcome with the feeling she knew something about me.

It was simple paranoia, of course. It was the sort of thing Cecilia Hyde had probably experienced, the little invasions of her mind, before they'd *become* her mind and she'd let slip her hold on reality. I stamped down on the thought. I needed to calm down. It was a tour, for Christ's sake. Was I so accustomed to the role of motherhood I'd let this office beat me down in only a few minutes?

Fuck. No.

"I've heard a lot about you," Zora said, with an insinuating smile. "Your interview, I mean. I heard you did fantastic."

"Grace, yeah?" the man at the desk next to her said. "I'm Derrick. You need anything sorted, like your computer breaks down or anything, come and ask me, yeah? I'm the Jack of all trades around here."

This came from a lean young man, probably in his mid-twenties – except for Clive, this place was making me feel absurdly old – with a skin-fade haircut and a confident smirk. He was fit and knew it, with his tucked-in shirt and his sleeves rolled up. He stared rather lasciviously, almost leering. It was like he was playing a porn video in his mind: fix her computer, bend her over the desk, pull down her tights, and *wham*.

"Right," Clive said. "Let's show you to your office."

"I get my own office?" I gasped, forgetting the vultures were still circling, Zora and Derrick, watching and mocking.

"Of course," Zora said, as though this was very obvious. "You earned it with all your *hard work*, no?"

There was an emphasis there I didn't appreciate. Derrick smirked and hid a laugh behind his hand. I tried to imagine why they could possibly be implying what they so obviously were: that Clive and I were in any way romantically involved. I looked at Zora and then Derrick, into their eyes, and I saw it again, the implication. *Where did you get that insane idea?* I thought, wondering if Clive had told them. But why?

"Ignore them," Clive said, as we walked away from what he called the Pen to the room directly next to his office. Floor-to-ceiling windows looked onto the Pen, but the blinds were shut. "They have a strange sense of humour. It's a bit like hazing. They like making the newbies feel uncomfortable."

I tried to believe him. "Okay."

But—

But what, Grace? But their eyes? You could look into the eyes of these strangers and immediately read their thoughts. Do you have any idea how you sound right now?

The office was elegantly furnished. A sleek desk in the middle, classier than the simple Ikea assemblies in the Pen. A small cream sofa sat off to the left, near a corner plant, with a glass coffee table in front of it. For a second I stared, a dumbfounded smile on my face, stunned this was mine, I'd earned this. I wanted to drag Mia and Russ in here and show them what Mummy had earned.

But I was Mrs Businesswoman today.

"It's very nice."

"All right, eh? Not the Ritz, but it'll do. Anyway, if you wait here, Olivia will come and handle the contracts. Sound good?"

"Um, yes." *That was the last time you say "um" in this building.* "Thank you."

He left and I walked around, feeling suddenly self-conscious. If I claimed this chair surely the motherhood patrol would come barrelling through the door, perhaps a woman wearing tight leather and a stern matronly expression. She'd point a whip at me and scream, "Get your arse back in the house this *instant*, young lady. Who do you think you are, playing with spreadsheets when you should be playing with Legos? Urgh, in my day..."

I was grinning at the absurd thought when somebody cleared their throat behind me. I turned to find Olivia, the rather distant woman who'd walked me to Clive's office for the interview. This time, she was smiling, her freckly cheeks made charming with the expression. Her eyes were kinder than before. She wore her red hair in a bob.

"Grace." She beamed, striding in her heels, a good two inches taller than mine. She balanced like a gymnast. "Why don't I give you the contracts and then I'll go and get us some coffees while you read over them? I'll get them from the café across the street, the good stuff. What do you like?"

I was about to tell her I'd quit caffeine. Every time I drank coffee my heart hammered and sweat poured and I regretted the decision. But that was only because I wasn't used to it and, really, what were the chances of me working in an office and avoiding caffeine forever? There was also the matter of Olivia's new-found friendliness. I didn't want to come across as the high-horse-riding weirdo who was too good for hot drinks.

It was only coffee, for Christ's sake. It wasn't like I was injecting heroin into my eyeballs. "I'll have a latte, please."

"One latte it is." She smiled, placing a few pieces of paper on the desk. "Be back in ten, hon."

I returned her smile and looked over the contract. It was, as far as I could tell, what was to be expected. My working hours were from nine until half past two, which would give me time to make the school run. *Just.* The pay was incredible. Probation, my responsibilities, et cetera. The only standout section was concerning overtime, where it stated it was a necessity in this position, but the company would always strive to give me ample notice in these circumstances. It seemed reasonable. I signed it and left it on the desk.

Soon Olivia returned with the coffees, the same rictus smile on her face. "Here. I hope it tastes okay. The girl was mucking about with the machine a bit."

"I'm sure it's fine."

She sat with me. I realised I was sitting in the senior position, and it all seemed so funny.

Olivia saw me smiling. "A lot to take in?"

"A bit." I reached for the paper coffee cup.

"You'll get used to it. Focus on the work. That's all you can do. And try to get as many hot drinks down you as possible. Cheers."

She raised her cup and I did the same, and then I took a large sip of the latte. It was good, so good. It was like manna from heaven. It settled on my tongue and then I felt it.

The kick. *Ah yes. Here we go.*

I drank more. Caffeine swam like electricity through my body. I found myself smiling, confidence filling me, and right then, sitting there with my new friend, I knew I could do it; I could do anything. I'd pushed two human beings out of my body. This was easy work in comparison.

"Enjoying that?" Olivia laughed.

"It's the most delicious thing I have ever tasted."

She laughed again and then I was laughing. It felt good to let go, to not be wound tight all the time, to not be like Mother. Holding it in. Waiting for it to explode.

Once I'd left the office, I felt too wired to drive. I wandered the city, ending up in the centre, strolling around Cabot Circus and peering into the shops. I imagined myself walking into one and getting anything I wanted, casually, a flick of the wrist with my card in my hand. Contactless, *beep*, and it would be mine. No thought of the balance.

I caught sight of myself in a shop window, but for a split second I didn't recognise the woman.

Usually I pricked with self-consciousness when I studied my reflection. I needed to go to the gym more. I needed to eat less. I needed to hate the way I looked because I used to be younger, thinner, shinier. And yet this woman looked like she didn't give a damn, owning her natural curves and the way her heels shaped her calves. Her hair was bright yellow and radiant.

She looked powerful. She looked sexy and dangerous. She looked like a person I wanted to be.

12

I gave Russ the biggest smile I could muster when I picked him up from school, ignoring the caffeine-induced hammering that went all through my body, seeming to persist rather too long. But never mind. Here was my son, finishing his first full week at school. It was a happy day.

When I asked him if he'd had fun, he shrugged and walked over to the car, where Mia was waiting. I looked back toward the school, the milling parents, the children springing all over the place, and tried to spot Naomi Mathieson through the fray. Every day I'd waited for her to tell me we needed to have another chat. But so far Russ's behaviour had been acceptable, if not exemplary.

I was glad, even if it meant my son seemed less like himself. "It's school," Troy had said a couple of nights ago, stroking his hands idly through my hair as we lay in bed. "It's bound to be hard. He'll get over it."

Part of me didn't want him to have to get over anything. I wanted him to flourish, to never be unhappy or bored, but of course that was unrealistic. Who enjoyed all their days, all the time? I couldn't be one of *those* mothers, the doters, the over-carers, the nothing-is-your-fault women whose children ended up robbing banks because they assumed the money within was rightfully theirs. If I went too far down that road perhaps Russ would get *Mummy* tattooed on his bicep in prison. Better to be tough.

"Are you excited to have dinner at Grannie and Grandpa's?" I said, backing out of the parking space and guiding the car toward the end of the road, where I'd start inching us toward Clifton. I wished – as I always did when I made this drive – my parents had moved after Hope's death. Driving up the hill was like driving into the past.

"Yeah." Mia rested her forehead against the window. "Is Dad coming or is he working?"

"Working. Sorry."

"It's okay. I hope Grandma has some more paintings for me."

I squeezed the steering wheel too hard. *Your daughter is obsessed with the visual rantings of a troubled woman.* I made my smile even wider, listening as she talked about how her teacher had complimented her today during art. He'd said she was getting a real eye for perspective, and had even called her a prodigy.

"Do you know what that means, Mum?" she asked.

"No," I lied.

Thump. Russ kicked the back of my chair and I pretended not to feel it.

Traffic had come to a stop. There was no space to go around; both curbs were covered in parked cars.

I was finding it hard to focus on everything at once.

Thump.

Russ certainly wasn't helping.

"...I'm going to be something one day," Mia finished. "Do you think he's right?"

"Of course." I ground my hand on the steering wheel, my heartbeat pounding as I waited for Russ to kick my chair again.

This time he did it with both feet, a full-throttle effort.

I spun on him quickly. "Russ, stop kicking my seat. It's annoying and it makes me want to shout at you, which I have no desire to do."

He lifted both legs, never breaking eye contact, bringing his knees to his chest as though getting ready for another kick.

"Russ," I warned. "I mean it. What's wrong? Did something happen at school?"

"I hate school," he whined. "I hate school and I hate *you*."

At the corner of my vision, I saw Mia's mouth open, the shock of Russ's words moving through the car like a rotten odour. Russ, my baby, my boy, always so polite and loving – everybody said he was a mummy's boy – and he hated me, he fucking hated me. My heart was drumming and my whole body was tingling, everything screaming at me to grab him, shake him, to make him pay for hurting me so badly. I squeezed the edge of the seat so I had something to hold on to, digging my fingernails in.

Then I saw Russ had tears in his eyes and Mia was looking at me in real horror, as though I'd crushed a baby's fragile skull with my heel.

Because I was shouting; I was screaming at my son.

I had to focus past my rage to hear the words. My throat was sore. "...You'll go to school through every holiday if you keep on, young man. Christmas, Easter, summer, all the half terms, say goodbye to them. I'll ask Miss Mathieson to give you extra homework and keep you after school. Would you like that? Well, would you?"

"N-no," he said, tears streaking his cheeks.

"No," I said, taking a breath, getting a hold of myself.

I never snapped so viciously. I couldn't remember a time

when my rage had been so easily accessible, so close to the surface.

Liar, a voice hissed. *As if you've always been so calm and kind. As if you've never snapped.*

I pushed the voice away. I pushed the past away. This wasn't about that.

I felt amped up and ready to get things done, that was all. And right now the thing I needed to accomplish was to stop Russ from acting up. I couldn't let him embarrass me in front of Mother. It worked in the sense he didn't kick my chair for the rest of the journey. But neither did Mia tell me more about her teacher's praise.

In fact, nobody said a word until we pulled up outside the house. It didn't feel like a victory. I felt like I'd gone too far and I didn't like it.

"I'm sorry, Russie," I said. "Mummy shouldn't have shouted."

"It's okay." He pawed at his cheeks, though they were dry. "I'm sorry too."

"Great. Then we're both sorry. I love you."

"Okay, Mummy."

My belly dropped. Of course he wasn't going to tell me he loved me. I'd screamed at him. What sort of mother was I, turning full berserker?

I turned to the house. My childhood home. I looked past the tree in the front garden to Hope's room, the one that fronted the street. With the lights off, all I could see was the reflection of the glass, a shimmer, and for a moment, a smile, utter glee in the twist of her lips.

I shook my head and reached for the door handle. "Come on. Let's not keep them waiting."

13

I'd felt like a stranger in this house ever since I'd returned from the police station to ostensibly sleep, but really to lie in bed and stare at the ceiling. I was convinced if I closed my eyes I'd dream too deeply and disappear into that evening, reliving it over and over again, seeing Hope's bike wheel spin around and around and...

Father was waiting in the hallway. Nicholas Addington was a sturdy seventy-year-old, with a head of thinning grey hair. He was perpetually dressed in Marks and Spencer's sweaters and chinos and shoes. "Grace," he said, striding over to me and opening his arms. "It's so nice to see you. Congratulations on the job."

I gripped onto him too fiercely, perhaps because I knew what was waiting for me when I greeted Mother. The look in her eyes: the frigid detachment. The buried hate. *It should have been you instead.* Even though Father had always felt uncomfortable around me since that evening – I knew I could never be the same in his eyes – he always made an effort, and I loved him for it.

"Your mother's in her office," he said. "Why don't you let her know you're here and I'll show these two my latest masterpiece? How does that sound, huh? You guys want to see the biggest model ship in the universe?"

"Woah," Russ said, laughing. I was glad he'd seemingly forgotten my tirade in the car. "It's really the biggest?"

"You bet it is. Come on."

I walked down the hallway, through the kitchen and into the garden, across the well-tended lawn and to the squat brick building at the rear. When Mother and Father first moved here, Mother had proclaimed her desire to become a writer. She'd failed long before I was born, apparently, though Troy told me writers never failed, they just stopped writing; getting a straight answer from one was impossible, evidently. It was an office in the sense it had a desk and bookshelves, but no work was done there.

Mother was sitting in her armchair in the corner, one leg folded over the other, looking like a skeleton with her bones showing through her face. Then I blinked, my eyes adjusted to the light, and I saw her through the dimness of the room. Isabella Addington was a devastatingly beautiful woman of sixty years, her hair sleek and white, her cheekbones well-defined. She wore a bright patterned dress and her hair was styled, which looked incongruous as she lounged there, reading *Great Expectations*, the paperback worn with time.

I couldn't make out the cover in the semi-darkness, but I knew the book well: the broken spine, the exact size and shape of it. It was the thief of my mother's attention in the years after Hope's death. I wondered if she could see the text, or if she recited from memory, silently singing the words in her mind.

My mother had dealt with being an ignored in-the-way child by losing herself in the books with which her cold academic father had stocked his library. The evening Hope died I saw her pick up a paperback, the same one she was reading now, and stare fixedly at it, refusing to look away. It was as though she could escape, like she did when she was a girl. She didn't have to deal with the madness of life.

"*Great Expectations*," I said from the doorway. "How many times have you read that now, Mother?"

"I'm sorry?" She raised the book like a shield, peering over the top of it, her eyes piercing with the rest of her face hidden. "Did you say something? I was utterly immersed."

"It doesn't matter. Father wanted me to let you know I was here."

I sound like a small scared child. How does she always do that to me?

"I can see that. I'll be in in a few minutes. Could you please ask Nicholas to get the beef out of the fridge? I want it room temperature. I'm making risotto."

"Yes, of course. I'll tell him."

She turned back to her book. I stared at her, wanting to tell her I got the job, but she already knew that. Father knew so she knew. But she hadn't said anything.

I lingered, waiting, watching as she slowly turned the page. The crisp papery noise seemed absurdly loud. Even if she were to ask me what I was doing, why was I hanging around, that would be something. She kept reading.

I left the room and quietly closed the door. I didn't want to disturb her more than I already had.

14

It was impossible to escape my sister in the dining room. As the five of us gathered around the table, she stared from three separate photos. She was smiling in this one, scowling playfully in that one, and staring in the third. I'd always hated the third: the way she gazed, dead-eyed, as though they'd taken a photograph of her corpse.

As a girl I was glad they'd rarely made us sit in here to dine, not after Hope left us. On the occasions they did – when Father had people over from work – I'd tortured myself with Hope's voice. I'd imagined her words, her voice, in my mind, coming from three separate places.

I'm coming to get you, she would whisper. *I'm riding on my bike and when you hear the wind, it's not the wind, Grace, no, it's my tassels rustling, my stupid fucking bike making a rustling noise. I'm coming to get you, big sister.*

I sat and waited for Mother to bring the plates in. I wanted to help her, but the few times I'd offered she'd given me this look, as though the very idea of needing my help was obscene. So I sat, watching Russ and Mia, trying to detect if my outburst in the car had mentally scarred Russ. But when I smiled he smiled back, and it meant a lot.

Mother and Father, not *Mum* and *Dad*, that was what I called Isabella and Nicholas Addington. It had not always been like that. In the graveyard silence following Hope's death, I didn't call for their attention for half a year. I didn't shout down the stairs asking what time dinner was. I didn't ask for money. I didn't talk to them unless they addressed me first.

Then one afternoon, in a mad bid to reclaim our family, we were at a restaurant and they were both sitting there like zombies. Outwardly, they were a presentable upper-middle class couple who'd had their only child later in life. Father in his salmon sweater and Mother with her pristine pearls. But their eyes were empty. They gazed out the window as the waiter approached, at nothing, or maybe at things only they could see.

When the waiter spoke to them, they continued staring, comatose. He looked at me – a cute older boy then, a spotty teen in hindsight – as if to ask what their problem was.

"Mother," I said. "Father. The waiter."

I was so embarrassed, convinced the whole restaurant was laughing at us. And there it was; they didn't correct me. They'd been Mother and Father ever since. If I'd called them by their first names at that dinner table, I was sure they'd be Isabella and Nicholas. If I'd remained silent and sat in the awkwardness, perhaps I wouldn't be calling them anything at all.

Mother brought the food in and I poured everybody pop and water from the jugs already laid out, a task Mother allowed me with a curt nod. Mia spoke at length about her art, and my mother's face lit up.

"You're exceptionally talented," she said, fork balanced like a weapon between manicured fingers. "I truly believe art is as much nature as nurture, and you have both, Mia. You have the natural eye *and* the desire to improve. After dinner, why don't I show you some more of your great-grandmother's work?"

"Do you have to?" I said, surprised to hear the sharpness in my voice.

Caffeine, caffeine, look what you've done to me.

Everything was sparking under the surface.

"Of course not," Mother said. "It was only an idea. Good heavens, Grace, do you truly imagine that by looking at some paintings Mia is going to become like my poor mother? You have always been so paranoid."

She was right. I'd been hounded by the idea I'd inherit Cecilia's madness since I was a child. It might've had something to do with the way Father told me. Mother had spent the night screaming and crying and walking with frenetic steps around her bedroom, a rare outburst that was not to be repeated.

Something in her had exploded, some primal chord struck. Father and I sat in the hallway outside her bedroom, Father's eyes red with lack of sleep and whisky, looking down at the floor and never at me, not once. He told me the whole story: the suicide, the gruesome method. He told me, yes, but truthfully I think he was telling himself.

"Isabella saw it, saw *her*. Her father died a few years later. She was alone until we found each other. A smoky flat in London, a party filled with friends of friends. But we were apart for years after. I was working abroad. And then we reconnected, in the bookshop, the musty old place. I walked in and found her there, this gorgeous angel behind the counter. What a romance!" He inflated, then grew sombre. "This is hard for her. She's always lived too close to tragedy. It's not fair she has to suffer this. I can still see her, the skinny girl with the sharp smile, standing next to that window, the smoke from her friends' cigarettes curling around her. I can still smell those days."

Ever since I'd learnt schizophrenia often ran in families, I'd felt the dangerous hands of possibility tickling up my spine more than I cared to think about. I tried not to be dramatic about it.

Schizophrenia had been treated differently back then, especially in the cloistered community in which my grandparents lived. My grandmother had been devoutly religious, and her psychoses were encouraged by some of her friends at church. Worse, my grandfather had sometimes played cruel tricks on her, gaslighting her in the sickest ways. Things were different these days. There were treatments, medication, therapies; people could flourish in spite of the vicious illness.

I let Mother's comment pass without rebuttal. I didn't want to erupt again.

It didn't take long for Russ to play up. We were about halfway through our meal when he scooped up a big fork of risotto and aimed it at Mia, preparing to fling it at her. Mother's eyes snapped to her grandson like a reflex. "Young man, if you even think about behaving like an animal at my dinner table, you can wait outside until the rest of us are done."

She didn't raise her voice. She didn't seem angry. She stared coldly.

Amazingly, Russ listened. Something flickered in his eyes, he gave a cheeky smile, and then he went back to eating his food. I should've been glad, but it sent a nasty thought rioting through my mind.

I wasn't as good at motherhood as Mother. I had to shout. She told.

"Grandma," Mia said a few moments later. "Isn't it fantastic Mum got the job?"

"Of course." Mother glanced at a photograph of Hope, the one where she was sitting on her brand-new pink bike. "Your mother truly is an intelligent woman. She could have a doctorate in psychology, you know, but of course life has its ways of meddling with such things."

"Because I was born, right?" Mia said.

"No. Grace could have returned to her studies after your birth, or continued them while she was pregnant. People do that when they are truly determined."

I was a let-down. I was everything Hope wouldn't have been. I silently seethed, which was my speciality under this roof.

"I'm proud of her," Mia said, giving me a secret smile.

It was strange – or perhaps normal, and only new to me – but the older Mia grew, the more I felt like she was my sister, my co-conspirator. I smiled back and on the meal went, the minutes ticking by, the six dead eyes of my little sister staring unceasingly.

Later, Mother took Mia to her office to peruse some of Cecilia's paintings. Russ and Father and I went into his workshop so he and Russ could work on his HMS *Victory*.

There were no photos of Hope in here, but there was a piece of her.

On the wall – beside the magnetic tool panel – hung a bracelet of small painted stones and seashells. I remembered sitting on the beach, feeling very grown-up as I sunbathed and waited for the boys to be impressed with my new swimsuit, as Hope skipped across the rocks, searching for the right size, the right shape, the right everything. It was the last bracelet she'd ever made.

15

My first week at Langdale Consulting was a frantic rush of events.

Even if I'd somehow passed the interview, I felt like an imposter as I strode into the office, into *my* office. As I set out my things on the desk, I found myself wishing I was with Russ in the park or at home or at the museum or anywhere else. Taking my seat, I forced thoughts of escape from my mind. I was here. I could do this. I'd be the best goddamn PA I could be.

"Don't expect me to coddle you," Clive said that morning, leaning against the wall with his arms crossed in a way that hid his paunch and showed off his Rolex at the same time. I wondered if it was intentional. "Management consulting is all about making them feel like absolute shit. That's lesson number one. The client, they're fucked. Beyond fucked. They're on the verge of bankruptcy. And only you can save them. That's what we need them to believe, all right? The hard part is having them still like you once you drop the bombshell. Sound cut-throat? Maybe so. But I'm throwing you in at the deep end, Grace. It's sink or swim at Langdale Consulting. And I expect you to be an Olympic-grade swimmer, okay?"

You're quite annoying, Clive.

"Of course," I told him. "I'll do my best."

"Give me one-hundred and ten per cent and we'll be gravy."

Clive spoke entirely in clichés, it seemed to me at times, but that was hardly my biggest concern. The first week was a battleground of catching up to something I had no experience in: writing reports, attending client meetings, learning how to play nice when one client called me a "good girl". All through it, my heart was a pounding drum in my chest, which might've had something to do with the coffees Olivia brought me twice or sometimes three times a day.

I didn't have the heart to turn her down. Or perhaps the caffeinated glory was the only thing getting me from nine until half past two, when I finished... or was supposed to finish. Twice during the first week, I had to ring Father to pick the children up from school, as unexpected overtime kept me tethered to the desk.

I came to look forward to the stolen minutes with Olivia, who seemed friendly if a little standoffish, as though she was unwilling to sink freely into a full friendship with me. It might've had something to do with the general atmosphere in the office, the sense I'd done something nefarious or immoral to get this job. I often felt as though my colleagues thought I'd had some prior relationship with Clive. Perhaps I was one of *those* women who slept with men to get jobs.

Or perhaps it was all in my head.

Perhaps, perhaps, perhaps. How I hated that word.

"How do you think I'm doing?" I asked one afternoon, taking another sip of the unbelievably strong coffee, as though the trendy hipster café had accidentally filled my cup with narcotics.

Her impish eyes glimmered knowingly. "Jeez, woman, don't worry so much. You're doing fantastic. I saw the way Tim Richardson was grinning when he left yesterday. You know how to handle people. And it's your first week. Honestly, I should resent you for doing so well. On my first week I could barely work the flipping scanner."

I laughed, letting her words bolster me, and then looked at the family photo I'd placed on my desk. The four of us were standing next to Wimbleball Lake in Exmoor, our faces ruddy from the cold, our expressions free and serene. I was doing this for them.

16

Derrick paused in the doorway of the break room. When he saw we were alone he smirked and stood up straighter. He was wearing gym gear, the fabric baggy and airy, giving him a careless handsomeness that somehow bothered me. As far as I could tell, he was the only one who made use of the in-office facilities.

"Hard at work?" he asked, with surface-level politeness.

The kettle hissed and finished boiling, bubbling loudly, and I thought about grabbing it and throwing it at him. It was glass and I knew it would make a satisfying shattering noise as it smashed over his shaved sanctimonious head.

"Just taking a short break."

"You deserve it." He beamed. "How is Clive treating you anyway? Hope he isn't hammering you too hard. I know he can be quite stiff sometimes. But sometimes you gotta lie down and take it, right?"

Hard-edged flaring, a whelming of violent intent inside of me. "Excuse me?"

I wanted to slap him so hard his teeth shattered.

Who the *fuck* did he think he was? I felt like a teenager, the lost version of me flashing into my thirty-year-old psyche. It didn't help that my heartbeat was a nonstop jackhammer and my thoughts were racing endlessly, always, around and around like—

Not now; not here. This was about him.

I strode closer. I lifted my chin. "As you've worked here longer than me, Derrick, I'm sure you're aware this company has a human resources department, as all modern companies do, and I'm also sure you're aware this is the twenty-first century and not the nineteen-fucking-fifties, so if you could keep your perverted thoughts to yourself, that would be very much appreciated."

"Woah." He blinked slowly, looking a little like Russ when he'd been caught sneaking a treat from the cupboard. "I meant with the workload. Hammering you with the workload."

"And lie down and take it?"

He was blushing. "The workload. Lie down and take the workload..."

"Of course that's what you meant," I scoffed, striding from the room, annoyed I'd had to abandon the coffee.

"I really did," he called after me. "I'd never say anything like that."

I walked quickly to my office and closed the door behind me.

I couldn't help but wonder if the comment *had* been innocent. Perhaps I'd overreacted. It was difficult to know. But it was over. Nobody had seen except for Derrick, and I doubted he'd be in a rush to repeat it.

You hope. Or he'll go around the office telling everybody how crazy you are.

"We're one big happy family here," Clive often said.

It was his mantra, but I was starting to doubt it already.

It didn't matter. I kept my head down, and soon it became clear Derrick had kept our scuffle private. He even directed a strange frown at me a couple of times, almost like he was upset, or regretful, or *something*. But it passed too quickly for me to read and I never acknowledged what had happened in the break room, even when we were forced to interact for work-related tasks.

It was almost like it had never happened.

17

I couldn't sleep, not properly, perhaps three or four hours a night, and even then it was never all at once. When I woke I was always covered in sweat and my first thought was to drag myself downstairs and make another coffee.

"She really has it in for me," Troy said when I returned to the bedroom one night, the house silent but for the creaks and whines of its settling. He was staring at his phone, the email app open, shaking his head. "What did I ever do to you, Vicky? Jesus Christ."

Vicky, his boss. It was always something. I had started to expect at least twenty minutes of ranting an evening.

I've already put in my time today, I unfairly thought as I sat on the edge of the bed. Without prompting, he told me the tale of Vicky and her order to have a stack of unreasonable reports ready for lunchtime the next day.

After several minutes of complaining, he looked at the digital clock, the red readout telling us it was one minute past two. "Jesus, listen to me. We better get some sleep. I'm sorry, Grace. I didn't mean to unload."

"That's what spouses are for, aren't they?" I teased. "Unloading all your woes and heartaches?"

"Yeah, maybe." He sighed, not taking the banter-bait. "But it's not fair. This is *your* week. It's going all right there, yeah? Clive's treating you well?"

"Everything's fine." I slid into bed next to him and snuggled close to his chest. "And everything." I kissed his cool skin. "Is going to be." I kissed higher, his neck, his beard. He laughed and so did I. "Fine. All right?"

We fell into each other's arms, but simply to hold each other. I hoped he couldn't smell the coffee on my breath.

Everything's going to be fine, I whispered into the cluttered fray of my mind, as Troy's breaths turned sleepy.

If Derrick or my insomnia or anything else became a real problem, I'd talk to him. We'd always been honest with each other. We'd always had long conversations about our relationship, our lives, our trajectory. Of course there were unsaid things, accepted silent things, like his truncated writing ambition and the fact he slightly resented me for my so-called posh parents, whereas he'd been born to working-class George and Phoebe.

But I wouldn't let my workplace stress become one of those Unsaid Things.

I promised myself.

And we all know how much your promises are worth, a bitter voice laughed within.

18

Russ troubled me that first week. He moped before school, dragging his feet to the table for breakfast. It was as though somebody was sucking the energy out of him, an invisible demon come to syphon my son's enthusiasm. When I asked if anything was wrong one evening – while he was building a giant dinosaur on Minecraft – he shook his head and kept his eyes glued to the screen.

"Russ," I said firmly.

"Wanna build my dinosaur, Mummy. Can I? Please?"

I didn't have the heart to tell him no, the note in his voice was so tragic, so pleading. I let him have fifteen more minutes on the screen, but not a second more. Later I read to him from his favourite book and ended up falling asleep on his bedroom floor. When I woke it was with my son's hands pawing at my shoulders.

"Mummy," he said.

It was the way he said it, how young he sounded, as if a two-month-old had learned to speak. I knew without asking that he'd wet the bed. I changed his sheets and told him it wasn't his fault, and held him until he fell slack and carefree in my arms.

Russ hadn't wet the bed in almost a year. Was there a problem? Should I be worried? Not according to Miss Mathieson. I stole a few minutes with her after school one afternoon, to be sure he was doing okay, he was making friends, he wasn't the weird kid with the dead little sister who tried to win approval by going too far with boys and being mean to girls, he wasn't—

Quiet, Grace.

"Russ is doing much better," Naomi told me, smiling in a way that seemed genuine. I sensed we were silently agreeing to ignore any awkwardness from the previous week. "His behaviour has been fantastic, actually. I should eat a big old slice of humble pie for overreacting before. But I do like nipping these things in the bud, if you know what I mean?"

Of course, yes, I knew what she meant. Better safe than sorry. I'd have to watch Russ, though, and make sure she didn't nip his joy for life entirely out of his personality. But change was what happened when children started school, everybody told me: Troy, Mother, Father, even my best friend, Yasmin. It was expected.

Life was a maelstrom with the job and the children to contend with, but I was making it work the best way I knew how. I woke on Friday morning with an unashamed feeling of accomplishment, almost enough to shoo away the sleeplessness, the *boom-boom-boom* of my heart. I'd almost done it, a full week of going out into the world and proving Grace Dixon still had a little Grace Addington in her.

That morning, Clive knocked loudly on my door and then swaggered in. That was always his way. A knock and then he was in my face, aiming the cloud-white smile that didn't quite match the wild dog in his eyes. "Grace, big ask. Next week I'm going to need you to do some overtime. You'll be well paid, obviously. But frankly, it's a weird request."

19

"Knock, knock," Olivia said, popping her bob of red hair around the door. "I come bearing lattes. I thought you might need an extra pick-me-up before another evening in the trenches."

Behind her, the office was a hubbub of sound as the rest of the Langdale Consulting team got ready to go home to their partners or pets or hobbies. It was Wednesday and I'd be spending it how I'd spent yesterday evening and Monday: sitting in this office on my own, trying to convince myself what I was doing wasn't a complete waste of time.

"Thank you," I said, as Olivia placed my flask on the desk; we'd decided to ditch the paper coffee cups and go eco-friendly. I could smell the coffee as steam rose through the small cracks between the lid and the flask, ghostly temping tendrils. "You really are too good to me."

"It's nothing. I think you need at least one ally in this place. God knows, it can be a flipping snake pit at times."

"Fine, but you must let me make the coffee run more often."

For a moment, it was almost like she was offended. Her upper lip twitched and a flash of pure hatred crept into her eyes.

She stared at me like I'd slapped her. Then it passed. Had I imagined it? Why would she resent me returning the favour? "I don't mind," she said.

"The coffee certainly does taste better when you get it." I laughed, trying to push away the nonsense paranoia fluttering around my mind. It was the truth. The coffee seemed to have an extra *oomph* when it was Olivia's turn.

"How are you finding it anyway?" she asked, hurrying the conversation along.

"Hand-copying reports from Word documents like I'm some sort of prehistoric barbarian?" I shook my head as a familiar wave of disbelief washed through me.

Hand-copying documents.

It was ridiculous.

"Clive's had a lot of eccentric clients over the years." Olivia shrugged but I could detect a note of suspicion in her voice. "Whatever you can say about him, he knows how to network. I guess if you meet enough people, eventually you'll find some crazies." *Like me.* "So yeah, good luck."

"Thanks," I replied. "Any plans for the evening?"

"Seeing my mum."

"Have fun."

She frowned. "Yeah, I will."

"Olivia, is something wrong?" I said, seeing the pain in her eyes. "I'm sorry if I offended you somehow."

"No, it's not your fault," she said. *It is your fault*, that ceaseless voice mocked. "My mum's got dementia, early-onset. She's only sixty."

"Jesus." Dementia, a sickness of the mind. New memories dying and old ones resurfacing. It terrified me. "I'm so sorry."

She looked at me silently for a short moment, as though judging if my words were sincere. It seemed like she wanted them *not* to be, her expression twisted into resentment, as

67

though she thought I was responsible for her mother's dementia. She reminded me of the cold Olivia who'd introduced me to the office.

But then it passed, and I was left wondering if I'd imagined the whole thing. *What whole thing? A half-second look? Get a grip, Grace.*

"Thank you," she said. "And try not to go too crazy this evening."

I laughed, but her words left me with a chill. I'd been spending my entire life trying not to go crazy.

I pushed it all from my mind and checked in with Troy and Russ and Mia, who were eating an actual meal instead of the microwave curry I'd nuke in about an hour's time. All was fine on the home front, so I had no excuse not to crack on with my absurd work.

"He's very particular, Grace," Clive had explained, when outlining my overtime for the week. "He's... ah, shit, what do you want me to say? He's cuckoo. For whatever reason, he prefers to read reports that have been hand-written, not typed out. I once tried using a hand-written font instead, you know, the fancy-pants ones people use on wedding invitations. No dice, Grace, no dice. But I thought: why not use this to our advantage? So I've managed to convince him to hire us for his next project."

Clive seemed pleased with himself, chest puffed up.

"It's easy work," he went on. "I know it's not glamorous, but who else can say they get paid your wage for rote copying?"

He was right, and though I was technically free to turn down the overtime, it was my second week and I didn't want to make a bad impression.

The reports were long and dull: workplace conduct regulations, paragraphs upon paragraphs outlining the correct procedure should a fire alarm go off, emailing etiquette, et cetera. I felt like I was in school, mindlessly copying from the board, having to write slowly so my script was attractive and not the usual quick scrawl I used for shopping lists and fridge notes.

I consoled myself with the fact there were people all over the world who'd kill to get paid for what I was doing. Fine, it was a little strange, a little *out there*. But so was Clive's approach to business.

But then my pen faltered and it wasn't from the cramp biting up my forearm. I'd come across a section titled "Guilt and Culpability". I tried to tell myself I was being silly as the words cast some bizarre spell on me.

"Those responsible for workplace malpractice will often try to rewrite the narrative," it read. "They will pretend they are the victims. Or they behaved far better than they truly did. Some will go so far down this road they will actually convince themselves they haven't done anything wrong. These are the most dangerous employees, the wilful blind, the indignant wrongdoers. These people can be car collisions for a business."

Was it the reference to car collisions, triggering images of Hope, poor innocent Hope? Why wouldn't they say car *crashes* instead, the most common metaphor? Car *collision*, well, that could be a hit-and-run, couldn't it? Perhaps whoever had designed this report – this report about *guilt*, for Christ's sake – had done so with the intent of sending me a secret—

"One," I croaked, forcibly placing my hands in my lap and slowing my breathing, which was assailing me rather too frantically. "Two, three, four..."

I counted steadily to ten. This was a coping mechanism I'd started in my teens when the panic attacks had become so bad I was afraid I'd be hospitalised one day. How would that look for Mother and Father? Not only had they lost one daughter, but another was unspooling. Using the steady breathing and the counting, I'd slowly gone from burying my face in a pillow and weeping and screaming to sitting like an effigy and waiting for it to pass.

I breathed; I counted.

In the months following the hit-and-run, Mother and Father didn't notice me walking like a ghost through the house at all hours of the night. They didn't see me writing *It's not my fault* over and over in a notebook until I couldn't close my fist from the tension. Perhaps they didn't care if I disappeared for an entire Saturday to sit at her grave and cry and pray I could hear her voice, pray I was mad or magic or anything, anything so I could hear my little sister's voice.

It's not my fault, I wrote now, on a new page.

What the hell was I doing? I balled up the paper and threw it in the bin. I turned back to the report and made myself write out the words, ignoring the subtle needling in my chest. It was like somebody was lightly prodding my heart.

20

I got home at half past eight. After looking in on the children, I joined Troy in the bedroom. "Evening," I said, dropping onto the edge of the bed and reaching down to tear off my shoes. I was already missing my UGGs like a phantom limb.

"Another easy night?" Troy bantered, peering over his laptop screen.

I bared my teeth and mimed throwing my shoe at him. He held his hands up. "All right, all right." He chuckled. "If I could get paid for writing out some reports for an eccentric millionaire, I'd feel pretty damn blessed. That's all I'm saying. Who do you think it is? Alan Sugar? Maybe some Saudi oilman?"

"It's boring. And I've got no idea who it is."

"He's paying, isn't he? That's all that matters."

"I suppose so. Anyway, how were the kids today?"

"Fine, mostly."

"Mostly?" I asked.

"Russ had a little temper tantrum at dinner and said he wanted to live with your parents. But you know how it is. School stress. He'll get over it in a month or two."

"We're doing the right thing, aren't we?"

"What do you mean?" He half-closed his laptop.

"With Russ."

"Well, yeah," he said. "You should've seen Keith when he started school, the little shit. We're both talking to him constantly, right? We're making sure he can share his problems with us. I think that's all we can do for the first couple of months. Obviously if we think something else is going on, ever, then we'll step in and take action. But honestly I think by Christmas we're going to see the old Russ back again. And Grace..."

He trailed off, getting a particular expression on his face. It was one I could read easily after being married to him for so long. It said, *I want to say something but at the same time I don't want it to spawn an hours-long discussion in which I am punished for saying it. And I don't want to offend you.*

"Troy?" I slid up the bed to sit next to him.

"I think this is going to be as hard for you as it is for him. It's a lot of change for both of you. But it's only been a couple of weeks. So let's hunker down and get through it."

I suspected he'd been on the cusp of saying something else before he hesitated, or at least he was going to phrase it differently. A decade of marriage had taught us that sometimes it's the battles you don't fight that matter the most.

I ignored the ever-present anxiety rampaging around my body. "Yeah, you're probably right. I love him and I don't want—"

I was crying, somehow. The tears had erupted and they were streaming down my cheeks.

Troy pushed his laptop aside and cradled me to his chest, his arms wrapped lovingly around me. "It's all right, Gracie-kins," he sang, the same way he'd said it over the years when I broke down about Hope.

"I'm okay," I huffed. "I don't know what came over me."

They will pretend they are the victims.

"Is this just about Russ?" Troy asked, softly running his fingers through my hair. "Whatever it is, you can talk to me."

"I know," I said, laying my cheek against his. "I'm tired. That's all."

Once the tears had passed, I went into the en suite and took a scorching hot shower, focusing on the physical sensation of the water sluicing down my body and nothing else, not the reports, not the ever-present hum at the back of my mind. Nothing, just the water, just the heat.

I prayed sleep would come easier. But the moment my head sunk into the pillow I knew I was in for another toss-and-turn marathon. I couldn't find a comfortable position. The duvet became an enemy. The mattress was rock-hard in places and doughy in others.

In the end – after waiting for Troy to start snoring – I went down to the living room with my Kindle, sitting with my knees to my chest and turning to this month's book club read. *The Virgin Suicides.* It had been Mike Foreman's choice, which didn't surprise me. Despite his laddish exterior, his picks were always dark.

I lost myself in the world of the book, living in the words, reality drifting away. It was about childhood and death and sex and anger and hate, and as I read I couldn't help but think of Hope. By the time I reached the end, the hazy early-autumn sun was glowing through the curtains. I could hear Troy's alarm whining upstairs. I hadn't slept.

I went to make myself a coffee.

21

At various points in my life I'd had the distinct feeling I was being followed. In the early years after Hope's death, some twisted conviction had arisen in me it was my little sister; she was the one who caused the animal instinct to rise in me to get away, get away *now*. I'd learnt to ignore this feeling and recognise it for what it most likely was. My regret, my grief, my guilt.

It's natural to think Hope would be watching me, judging me. Of course it is.

But as I walked through Cabot Circus – to meet Troy for a hurried lunch – I felt it again, that prickling. It was a primordial sensation, a leftover from when this feeling meant a predator lurking in the underbrush, a big cat about to wrench me down into the dark. I strode and kept my head bowed, telling myself I was paranoid.

Lack of sleep could really mess a person up.

But then I turned and, hugging to the corner of a clothes shop with a baseball hat pulled low over their eyes, I saw them, him, a man. A man was standing there and watching me. I stared and my mouth hung open and all around me harried Bristolians sighed loudly with classic British reticence.

I was too far away and there were too many people bustling around for me to make out the features of the man's face. He was wearing a long-sleeved shirt and jeans, and as I watched he pulled the black hat lower and lifted his hand. He waved… at me? I couldn't tell. He waved and then turned away, disappearing around the corner of the shop.

"Excuse me," I was suddenly saying, pushing past people, elbowing them out of the way as my breath became loud and frantic in my ears. "Excuse me. Sorry. *Excuse me.*"

I remembered standing outside my halls of residence at university with this same feeling creeping over me. *You're being watched.* As I'd looked up at the end of the street, I'd spotted a man in a black baseball cap like this one was wearing. He'd lifted his hand and waved and then disappeared. At the time it was easy to chalk it up to him waving at somebody else. The world didn't revolve around me. But he'd returned. Who was he?

I jogged, and then my jog broke into a run and I was speeding around the corner. I spotted him. He was striding past Primark, which would lead him left onto Union Street, and then he could disappear onto Nelson Street or loop back around to Broadmead. The idea occurred to me, as I ran through the city – muttering apologies – I was chasing a stranger for no apparent reason.

The man in the hat turned and glanced at me, far too quickly for me to make out his face. *Who the fuck are you?* He could've been looking at me or he could've been looking at something else. I couldn't tell.

I pressed on.

The traffic lights betrayed me and a river of pedestrians crossed at the exact right time for this man. He blended into the crowd and I was forced to slow, panting, tracking the blackness of his baseball cap as he walked down Union Street, and then disappeared onto Nelson. I broke into a run again, heels clipping, breath coming far too quick.

Was it possible I'd been physically fit once, Yasmin and I sitting on horseback with my legs fine-honed, my core solid with maintaining my posture? I felt my chest banging as I tried to catch up. I turned onto Nelson.

I couldn't see the man in the black hat, only a couple of teenagers smoking and leaning against the wall and the usual passage of pedestrians.

I stared, biting my bottom lip, chewing it until I felt blood prick and I forced myself to stop. There had *been* a man, hadn't there? If I were to check the CCTV – which of course I had no way of doing – I would see a man. Yes, of course I would. What I wouldn't see was a stressed overtired woman running through Bristol city centre chasing a phantom, nothing, the guilt that gnawed at her mind endlessly and the whisper at the edge of it all.

You know what you did. You don't want to know. But you do.

This was ridiculous. If I'd had a stalker who'd been following me for over a decade, surely I would've seen him more than twice.

If he had been following me all this time, why? It didn't make any sense. Perhaps my mind was conflating two separate incidents. The man at university had been waving at somebody else. And this man, this so-called watcher, he'd also been waving at somebody else and had happened to turn and walk away as I'd started to run. Perhaps I needed a good night's sleep. Perhaps I needed to take a few deep breaths and get myself together.

Or perhaps it was *him*—

"No," I muttered.

It wasn't him. I didn't even know who *he* was. Or even if he was a *him* to begin with. I'd had too much caffeine and not enough shut-eye and I'd made an embarrassing mistake, letting my nerves get the better of me.

I wasn't my grandmother. I wasn't mad.

"Excuse me," I heard myself say, calling over to the smoking teenagers. One was a girl with dyed pink hair and fishnet stockings, and the other was a boy with swept green hair and skinny torn jeans. They turned to me sluggishly, bored, already uninterested in what I had to say. "Did you see a man walk through here? Um, regular height, wearing a black baseball hat?"

The boy smiled, but it seemed mean somehow, cruel, like he was tricking me. Like he was in on it.

Quiet, Grace.

"No." He yawned. "I haven't seen anybody."

"Yeah, sorry," the girl said, smirking. "There ain't been any man. Why? You looking for someone?"

"You didn't see a man in a black baseball hat walk through here?" I snapped, fiercer than I'd intended.

Lying little shits.

"Nope," the boy said.

"I guess you missed him, then," I said, turning away and walking back up the street.

Of course they'd missed him. He was just another pedestrian. Why would they pay him special attention? But then surely he'd been moving quite quickly to make the distance between the turning onto Nelson Street and his disappearing act. Into a shop? Around the corner? Surely he'd been at least *jogging*. Wouldn't they have noticed that?

22

Clive strode into my office. He had a flustered look on his face and his shirt was loose around his hips and crinkled. He tried to smile at me, but I could sense the unhinged aura around him. "Grace," he said, sitting down opposite me, another indicator he wasn't his usual fake-faced self. He never normally sat down in my office; he'd loom over my desk, ever the CEO. "Sorry to barge in like this."

"It's fine."

He must've seen me look at his crinkled shirt, because he drummed his fingers on the desk and then said, all in a long rush, "Well, what're you going to do? I've never been much of a whizz with the iron and the lovely lady who's currently handling it for me has decided to give me the silent treatment. And do you know why? Get this. Because I didn't *stand up* to her ex-boyfriend, the father of her kid, which seems pretty fucking ridiculous to me. What does she want me to do, put on some boxing gloves and go at it with him? It's none of my goddamned business."

I watched and waited. He wasn't really talking to me, more to himself, and I just happened to be here. He waved at the air as though banishing the thoughts and then leaned forward, gripping the edge of the desk.

"Anyway, I didn't come in here to complain. I wanted to ask if you'd be open to receiving work-related texts and calls after hours. I know, I know, I'm a cheeky bugger for even asking. It wouldn't be often. Maybe even ever. But when you tell your clients you're a twenty-four-seven kind of bloke, they come to expect it. Okay?"

The way he said it, I knew it wasn't a question. It was a formality. I wanted to tell him no, absolutely not, my time at home with my family was sacred. I wanted to shout at him for putting me in the position of having to say no. But Troy had been singing my praises more and more about the job lately, and I had to admit I did feel proud when Mia said I looked fierce in my work clothes. "Sort of like a lion, does that make sense, Mum?"

I enjoyed the battleground of Langdale Consulting, how it felt to stride into businesses around Bristol at Clive's side, my face as much of a mask as his normally was. Smiling, shaking hands, feeling fit and young and capable. Feeling intellectual. Feeling like I graduated from university, I didn't drop out after all, I could do it, do anything, ride up to the Houses of Parliament and be made Prime Minister if I wanted to. I was fucking *doing it*.

Before I knew it, Clive was moving on; he'd taken my silence as assent. I seethed. I was so damn good at silently seething.

"I've got another big ask," he said. "More overtime. Probably only a few evenings here and there. But the client who you're writing the reports for, well, he wants someone in the office in case he decides to ring."

"Can't he ring my mobile?"

"He's a fucking weirdo, Grace," Clive pushed on, as if I hadn't spoken. "I don't know what goes on in his head. But he's told me he might ring the *office* and if he does, he wants somebody *here* to pick it up. If we don't, he'll take his business elsewhere. I think he might be screwing with me, honestly. He has enough money he could do that if he wanted. But the joke's on him, right? He's paying."

"So I'd sit here and wait for a phone call that may or may not come?"

"Yeah. And get paid overtime money for doing it." He snorted. "It's a perfect job, right? I think I've told you before, don't look a gift horse in the mouth."

"Yes, you have said that before." In my mind, the man in the black hat watched me, shadowed face smirking. I pushed him away. Two days earlier, and the faceless bastard wouldn't leave me alone.

I tried to think of a reason to tell Clive no. But where was my leverage? There were hordes of beleaguered workers all over Bristol who would leap at the opportunity to sit in an empty office with their Kindle waiting for a phone that might ring. It was all absurd, but everybody here understood that; this client, whoever they were, was a Howard Hughes type, an eccentric with logic that only made sense to him.

"How long do you imagine we'll be working with this client?" I asked, my voice sharp and cutting, the voice of a woman who was getting two to three hours of sleep a night. And then pouring a whole Boots' counter on her face to hide the sleepless lines creeping into her skin. It was like having a newborn again, this sleep pattern, a perpetual exhausted haze. "Because although I am grateful for the overtime, I do find the whole arrangement rather strange."

"You and me both." I thought I saw rage flicker across his expression. Why would he be angry? For paying the overtime, maybe? "But he's a rich asshole and rich assholes get what they want."

So for two weeks it was that way: more overtime, more reports. I spotted three more references to car crashes and collisions in the reports I was hand-copying, but of course that was a coincidence, because there were several dozens of references I didn't pay attention to. *Once you get an Audi, Audis are everywhere.* It was perception bias; I'd read about it in university. It was no big deal. The phone didn't ring on the two evenings I sat in the office.

One cloudy morning, waiting for Olivia to return from the café with my blessed manna ("I'll get the real stuff, I won't be long, hon..."), I went to grab my phone to check if Troy had texted me. I normally kept it on the edge of my desk, next to the framed family photo. But it wasn't there. I searched my office.

Nothing.

Olivia returned with the coffees and we drank, and still there was no phone. Part of me wondered if Derrick had stolen it, his revenge for the exchange we'd had in the break room my first week here. Since then the office had felt even more unwelcoming. It was fast becoming the norm to sense the vultures watching me from behind their desks, waiting for me to stumble and fall so they could pick apart my body. But it didn't matter. I rarely had cause to set foot in the Pen. I was alone.

Later, I found my mobile on the floor. I was sure I'd thoroughly looked under my desk. But there it was. It made no sense. Why steal a phone and then secretly return it? Perhaps he'd tried to get into it and then realised it was password-protected. Or perhaps I'd missed it with my sleep-hungry eyes.

23

Returning home to find Troy beaming in his writer's cubby filled me with warmth. It wasn't often he looked so carefree these days, as though he'd fallen back ten years and was filled with the same unapologetic ambition that had first attracted me to him.

"What are you so happy about?" I dropped my handbag as I walked over. "Finally worked up the nerve to have an affair?"

"Ha, ha," he grunted. "Nope. I do have some big news though."

I nodded to the glass bottle on his desk, the air filled with its sweet scent. "It's a cider kind of revelation, is it?"

He rarely drank when the children were here, but Russ and Mia were at his parents' house in Weston-super-Mare, staying the evening as they did once or twice a month. We were lucky to have such a supportive network, I had to remind myself every so often; the steeliness with Mother sometimes blotted that from my mind.

"Well? Don't keep me in suspense."

He grabbed me and pulled me into his lap, his hand resting on my leg, sending shimmers up my thigh. "I've been emailed by a small independent publisher. They want to publish my novel, Grace."

But your novel isn't finished.

That was my first thought. Unfair, a reflex. I beat it down. Troy was an intelligent person and I doubted he'd make a mistake about something so important to him.

"They read my short stories online and they want a longer piece of work. They're willing to pay an advance, small, but a show of good faith, a show they're serious."

"That's great," I said, chest blooming with pride.

Maybe this was it. His big break. He'd waited so long.

"So what happens next?" My voice was getting giddy as I thought about all the heartache and rejection he'd experienced over the years. "God, Troy, I'm so proud of you!"

"I wait for them to send over the advance, and then I start work. I haven't got my head in the clouds here, my little worker bee—"

"Call me that again and I'll chop your bollocks off."

He wriggled against me, making my cheeks flush. "Noted. But until I see the moola, I'm not getting my hopes up."

I prodded him playfully. "You're getting your hopes up already, arsehole. I can tell. And why not? You've worked so hard."

"Can you imagine?" he said wistfully, hugging me tighter, while beyond the closed curtains and the low lamplight, a soft wind purred. "I'm not saying I'll do this straight away, obviously, but imagine, Grace, quitting my job, that goddamn hellhole. Writing for a living. It'd be... Jesus, I don't even know what it'd be. Surreal."

"You deserve it. I hate that you've had to put your dreams on hold for us."

"No, it's not like that."

We both knew it was a lie. It was exactly like that. Having a baby at twenty had never been part of the plan. But life happened and I knew Troy didn't regret Mia, not for a second.

"Anyway," he said. "Getting this good news has made me realise I've been a bit of a selfish dick about work over the past few weeks. I'm running you a bath, the works. Candles, bubbles, music, everything. And you're going to lie there with a glass of wine and do nothing but relax. Okay?"

"Okay," I said, moving closer to him, breathing in my husband's scent, feeling my heart pick up for an entirely different reason. "But first..."

We did it right there like savages, with the wild abandon we could only give into when the children were staying elsewhere. Bent over his desk, I pushed against him, savouring every shivering breath and groaning noise he made. We finished together, both of us shaking and roaring like mad.

Later, I lay in the bath, the warm water seeming to drag me down. Sleep came with difficulty these days, but that evening the water felt like it was weaving around me.

I slept, and I dreamed I was at the top of a hill in a lashing rainstorm, when the weatherman had promised sun, sun, fucking sun, and a little girl rode her bike down the hill and there was a crash, a whimper, and as I got to the bottom of the hill I turned and there was the car, and there was a figure stepping from the car, rain-silhouetted in the evening haze.

The figure raised a hand to the brim of his cap.

I awoke violently, lukewarm water spraying across the room.

It was just a nightmare, I assured myself immediately, banishing it from my memory. I'd never met the driver, never even seen a photograph. The devil's leer I sometimes saw in my darkest dreams was a cousin to the guilt I felt for being there that evening. I should've done more. The driver was still out there, a nameless criminal, a faceless killer. The police had tried – so very hard – but unfortunately they'd failed.

I remembered how calmly they'd questioned me at first, asking me if I'd seen anything, anybody, and how their calm had turned to something else later on, a well-concealed frustration I could nonetheless detect behind the surface emotion of their eyes. *It's really important you tell us everything. It could mean the difference between catching the person responsible and them going free.*

I climbed from the bath and stood there naked, shivering.

24

I sat on the bench in Queen's Square, the sun shafting through the trees despite the nascent cold, a hint of true autumn with winter riding on its back. People passed me, somebody walking a gorgeous pointy-eared dog with a tail that seemed to be attached to a motor, and when their owner waved at me, I smiled, a true, genuine, not-faking-it smile.

Despite everything, today was a good day. Mother had asked me to meet her for lunch, something which rarely happened. And it was my first payday.

I looked down at the mobile banking app on my phone again, still amazed at the number on the most recent transaction. Langdale Consulting had paid me almost twice as much as Troy made in a month, and that was my probation wage; in six months' time, it would increase. All the overtime, all the meetings, all the pretend smiling, all the small talk, it had paid off.

It might've been materialistic of me, fine, but I felt a whelming in my chest when I stared down at the number. I'd gone from earning nothing to earning more than Troy, and suddenly – perhaps selfishly – it all seemed worthwhile. I sat up straighter, wearing my blazer like chain mail.

I navigated to my internet app, went to my bookmarks, and opened the clothes website I'd been browsing a couple of months earlier. My basket was still saved. It was two hundred and ten pounds. I hovered my finger over the checkout button and felt giddiness running through me, as though I was doing something wrong.

You materialistic little bitch, a voice giggled in my head, drunk with sudden power, like a teenager after one too many cheap ciders.

I bought the clothes and then an art set for Mia. I bought Russ the trampoline he'd asked for the previous month. I bought Troy a voucher to a bookshop and then I forcibly shoved my phone into my handbag, reminding myself there were still bills and life to pay for.

"Oh, Grace."

I turned to find Mother standing on the grass behind me, dressed in her jogging gear. She met with a couple of her lady friends a few times a month to power-walk through the city, and I supposed she'd slotted our lunch date around that. Which was fine, I told myself. It didn't matter if I was an afterthought. At least I was a *thought*.

"It's so funny," she said. "I was thinking you must be an executive type, somebody important, you know, because you look so proper in your business attire. I didn't even recognise you. It's so refreshing to see you out of UGG boots."

She said it with her natural detachment, but the words were like a soothing balm. For so long, I'd wanted to make her proud, wanted her to say something, anything positive about me. And here it was, the validation I'd been seeking. I didn't care if it made me pathetic or needy or childish. I held on to it. Because I knew it was only a passing moment and probably didn't mean much – if anything – to her.

As we walked together to the café, I ignored the voice taunting at the edge of my good mood, the voice that told me the greatest thing I could be to Isabella Addington was a stranger on a park bench.

25

The feeling of control stayed with me for a week, a persistent buzz thrumming beneath everything I did. If I couldn't sleep, it was because I didn't *want* to sleep. I'd read instead. Or listen to music. It was time taken, not stolen. If my heart was a rave banging in my chest, fine, it was the best damned rave in England, the sort where lives were made and relationships were forged.

Insomnia was a gift of glorious time, I decided, time that let me binge make-up channels on YouTube and learn their art. I hid behind a mask of finely-sculpted features, using it more expertly than I ever had before. It didn't matter how my face really looked as long as outwardly I was fierce.

I was in charge of myself. I was in *charge*, full-fucking-stop.

If this was mania then it was the sort that was paying off. Even Clive, ever reticent with positive feedback, seemed impressed with me one day after a meeting with Timothy Richardson, one of our most finicky clients. Richardson had yet again failed to implement Clive's advice. He'd disregarded notes about restructuring and had failed to make ten per cent of his workforce redundant.

These were the cards we dealt with in Langdale Consulting: redundancy and disarray.

I leapt in when it appeared as if Mr Richardson was going to withdraw his business. "Then you should tell us to leave and never come back," I snapped, already standing as if I was going to march out.

His face collapsed. Beside me, I felt Clive tensing.

"Excuse me?" Richardson hissed.

"I said," I went on, resting my hands on the desk and staring him straight in the eye like the craziest bitch in the nuthouse, "if you're not going to take our advice, what's the point of us being here? It's like going to a strip club and staring at the wall, a rather fruitless endeavour, I think we can all agree. Your business is failing. It's already failed if you refuse to put your ego in check. You're drowning and instead of clutching on to the rope we're throwing you, you're strangling yourself with it. So, which is it to be? We're actually quite busy today, Tim, so if you have no use for us, we'll be on our way."

I stormed out, head held high.

A few minutes later, Clive emerged, a disbelieving smirk on his face. "Jesus Christ, Grace. You've got some goddamn stones on you."

I was shocked at the vicious way I'd spoken to Richardson, but then I hadn't always been the woman rooting around for colouring pens under the settee. I felt old parts of me emerging into my personality, aspects of myself that had collapsed under the weight of Hope's death. I felt confident and brand new. So what if we were basically fleecing Timothy Richardson? It wasn't our fault he paid us and then did the opposite of what we told him.

When Russ's trampoline arrived, I assembled it myself at half past six in the morning. With a light drizzle lacing the air and the security light guiding me, I grunted and sweated and then, when Russie woke up, it was there waiting for him.

"Mummy!" he yelled, bubbling with excitement. "Can I go on it before school? Please? Please?"

"Of course you can. But only if you promise to jump as high as you can, okay?"

"Daddy, look what Mummy did," Russ said when Troy came to the back door in his dressing gown.

"I told you I'd do that tonight." He looked at me like I was a new person. It reminded me of the first few weeks after the university party where we met. He'd had this glint of fascination then, as though he'd never tire of learning all the little details about me. "What's gotten into you lately?"

"You're saying you don't like it?" I laughed, grabbing him and kissing him hard.

"Mum," Mia said, staring bleary-eyed from the hallway. "Do you know how gross that is?"

"Mwah, mwah, mwah." I chased her up the stairs as she giggled and flapped her hands at me. We ended up on her bed, wrestling, until she remembered she was almost eleven and far too mature to be wrestling with her silly old mum.

Things kept getting better.

We danced around the kitchen when Troy received his advance from the small independent publisher: two thousand pounds, the most money he'd ever earned for writing by far. "Now I need to get on with writing the bloody book," he said good-naturedly.

He showed me the publisher's website as if to prove it was legitimate. It looked like any other website to me. And the money was evidence enough. It wasn't vanity publishing. They hadn't published many other books, but they wanted to invest in Troy. Somebody had finally realised how talented my husband was.

"I don't know how I'm going to juggle work and the book," he said one evening, leaning against the kitchen counter.

"So quit."

He recoiled as though I was radioactive. "Grace, be real."

"I am being real. All our lives, Troy, we've been living in fear. What might happen. What could happen. But this is it, your big chance, and we're in a situation where you can quit and I can support us. Anyway, it's not like you won't be working. You'll be working at what you love doing. It's your dream."

"You're serious, aren't you?" His voice caught with emotion. I knew he was already envisioning himself discussing this moment at a writer's convention. *I couldn't have done it without her.* "Are things at work really going that well?"

I grabbed him and kissed his stupid handsome goatee, and then wrapped my arms around him and sunk deeper into the kiss, feeling his desire flame in step with mine. "I want to do this," I said, breaking it off as suddenly as I'd started it. "I *can* do this. I know I can. Right now... God, I don't want to sound conceited. But right now I feel like I can do anything."

"You're not conceited." He brushed hair from my face. "I've always known you could conquer the world if you wanted to."

26

Vicky didn't protest when Troy put in his notice, which conjured up all sorts of paranoid theories in my mind about why she'd suddenly taken a disliking to him. Troy had had an affair with her and jilted her. Troy had been caught watching porn at work. Troy had tried to steal from the company. Troy had done all manner of underhanded or even illegal things. All nonsense, of course, but the confusion persisted.

Why does she hate you, Troy?

They'd seemed to get on okay for years. I'd seen them together at work functions and never detected any resentment, not until the past few months. But it was done. I'd made the offer on a high and when the low came it was too late to retract it. The notice was put in place. From the way Troy described it, Vicky was glad to kick him out the door.

One afternoon I googled the symptoms of caffeine addiction and found I fitted most of them. Restlessness, rambling thoughts, difficulty concentrating, a general feeling of fogginess... on and on, and, of course, my beloved insomnia.

When I looked back on the week of my first pay cheque and the way I'd glorified insomnia, I cringed.

Enough whining, I snapped at myself one afternoon, sitting in my office. *It's time to do something about this.*

I made a chart and decided I would track the number of coffees I drank in a day, but when the first day showed I'd consumed six, I lost my nerve. Then I decided I was taking all of this rather too seriously, becoming quite obsessive, in fact, and it was this – the obsessive thinking about caffeine – and not the caffeine itself that was driving me bonkers. Everybody consumed caffeine. It wasn't a big deal unless I made it a big deal.

Then I decided I was making excuses and I had to quit again.

About an hour later, Olivia came to visit me, wearing her usual impish smile and bearing her usual mug of lightning, which I drank because...

Well, *fuck it*. What was I, a monk?

Life was better than good and yet this sense of utter dread lurked over everything I did. In fits and starts I'd retrieve the feeling of power my first payday had brought. I kicked ass more than once, my reports were always professionally written and researched, and even if Zora and Derrick and a few others enjoyed intimating Clive and I had some sort of romantic relationship, they were gracious enough to keep their remarks veiled.

But the whispering voice would always return, telling me something was wrong, *I* was wrong. I'd have to face up to it one day.

"You're a demon, Grace," the man in the black hat told me casually one night, perched on the end of my bed as I lay pinned in sleep paralysis. I tried to move; my mouth wouldn't open to scream. He smirked and his teeth were bright in the dark and I knew this without looking, because it was a dream. *Wake up, Grace.* Or was I awake? "You'll realise that one day."

I stopped arguing with Clive about the overtime. Once Troy's final payday came and went I'd be the sole breadwinner. The thought had made me feel heroic at first. Now I felt a weight bearing down. This was how Troy had felt for the past ten years, I scolded myself.

The reports made more references to car collisions, but only here and there. Incidental. Buried. I saw them because I was looking for them. *A slippery road.* Did that count as a reference or was I reading too much into it? But then why say *road* and not the more commonly used *slope?*

On the evenings I had to wait for Mr Self-Important Dickhead to ring, the phone remained silent.

Russ wet the bed three more times over the next two weeks, walking silently into our bedroom and shaking me awake. He always watched Troy as he did this, as though ashamed his father would wake and discover what he'd done. I changed the sheets quietly and then held him, sometimes falling asleep in bed with him. I talked to his teacher again, but all was fine, she assured me. He was doing well.

Some children struggled with Reception. I wished people would stop telling me that, no matter how true it was.

Russ's Reception struggles spread through the house; one day I was taking a pasta bake from the oven and I heard a clattering noise from the dining room. I rushed in and found Mia had dumped all the plates and cutlery in the centre of the table. She usually took pride in setting the table, but now she sat with her head bowed, tears glistening in her eyes. Her closed fist rested on her knee and her other hand moved to her hair and smoothed it over her face.

"Mia." Terror stabbed me in the chest. Mia was the calm one. This was the equivalent of punching a hole in the door for her. I walked over and tried to place my hand on her shoulder, but she flinched away. "What's wrong?"

"Like you don't know," she scoffed. "Why don't you go and ask Russ?"

"Mia, look at me." She stared at the table, bottom lip trembling. "Please."

She slowly met my eyes. "I'm looking at you. Now what?"

"I promise I don't know what this is about."

"That makes it worse. It means I might as well disappear and nobody would even care."

I pulled up a chair, feeling like the worst excuse for a mother. I made to place my hand on her again and then thought better of it. I wanted desperately to smooth the tears from her cheeks, but I knew she wouldn't let me.

"Talk to me. You know you don't have to keep anything from us. Not ever."

"I shouldn't even have to say."

Wind howled outside. A memory struck: pressing my ear against the cold winter glass, wondering if I listened hard enough I'd be able to hear Hope's voice. I pushed it away. I'd been a confused teenager, grieving. Of course it was natural to have silly thoughts.

"If you don't tell me what's wrong," I said, some bite in my voice, "how are we supposed to discuss it?"

"Who said I wanted to discuss it?"

"Young lady, you're testing my patience."

Her shoulders slumped and she picked at the table with her thumbnail. "It's just it's all about Russ. If Russ has a good day at school then it's all about that and if he has a bad day it's all about that and... Mum, I'm not selfish. Really I'm not."

"I know." A sob tried to crack my voice. I swallowed it down. "You're the furthest thing from selfish."

"But it's not fair everything is about Russ all the time because this is his first year in school. I didn't cry like a stupid little baby when *I* started school."

"It's harder for him. Everybody's different. Some people take longer to adjust. But you're right. We haven't been giving you the attention you deserve and I'm glad you said something. Really, I am. I know what it's like to live in a house and feel like you're invisible and I'd never want to do that to you. I love you so much. The day you were born, it was the happiest day of my life. I felt like I'd spent all my life searching for something, and you were it."

I trailed off, realising I'd begun to cry. Mia looked at me with surprise and then she was the one to reach across and smooth the tears from my cheeks. "I'm sorry, Mum. I didn't mean to make you cry."

"You have nothing to apologise for. I don't want to make you feel unloved. I love you more than I could ever explain."

"I love you, too," she said, leaning across to hug me.

I savoured the moment, which was getting rarer as time went on. I held her tightly and inhaled the scent of her hair, the same way I'd spent hours breathing in the smell of her as a baby. Then we got up and starting setting the table together.

"Mum," she said, without looking up.

"Hmm?"

"Do you think things will go back to normal soon?"

"What do you mean?"

"Like with Grandpa picking us up from school so much."

"Well, your father will be picking you up every day from now on. He'll be working from home so he can fit it around his schedule. Don't you like it when your grandparents pick you up?"

"No. I mean, yes. It's..." She paused, glancing at me shyly, and then turned back to the table. "I like it when you pick us up."

I thought about what to say, but then I realised Mia wasn't waiting for a reply. She had wanted me to know how she felt. Now I did. And there was nothing I could do about it. In all likelihood, I wouldn't be picking them up from school for a long time. I'd spoken to Clive about getting more permanent full-time hours and he'd sounded optimistic. Even if this was something I should be proud of, it was hard not to think about everything I was losing.

27

I returned home from book club with tension tugging at every part of me. We'd read *The Virgin Suicides*, chosen by Mike, and the discussion of the book was driving a drill into my head. We'd had to push the meeting back by a couple of weeks; life had gotten in the way, like always. I'd thought the gap might make me forget the rawness of the novel. But talking about the deaths of the little girls, I couldn't help but let my mind stray to Hope, to the awful evening that would never leave me the hell alone.

Troy was on his computer when I walked into the living room, as he often was lately. Except instead of staring at a blank page, he was typing up a storm, orchestral music blaring loudly from his over-ear headphones. I stood in the doorway and watched him for a few minutes, brimming with pride.

"I needed that first glimmer of hope," he'd told me a few nights earlier. *Hope.* "I've got it, Gracie-kins. And nothing's going to stop me."

I went upstairs and looked in on Russ. He was already asleep, his nightlight showing me his pensive face. He'd looked so peaceful in sleep, once, but ever since school a new heaviness had come over him. He was slowly returning to his old self at home, but I knew it would be a long process. And he still disliked school. He hated maths. He hated English. He hated anything that didn't involve building or playing. I silently asked whoever was listening to let him be all right.

Mia was awake, sitting at her desk, her lamp reflecting off the glass of the photo frame. A tremor moved through me when I saw it was a school photograph of Hope, enthralling with her cheeky smile and her vivacious eyes, her signature braid draped over her shoulder. An insane thought spiralled into my mind. Mother had given Mia this photo to screw with my head, to drive me mad, because she hated me more than anybody, resented me for that rainy evening, and she wanted to torture me, to make my hold on reality as tentative as her own mother's had been, before—

Quiet, Grace.

Mia turned. "What do you think, Mum? Do you think it's good? Or is it terrible? I don't even know."

I strode over to the desk, telling myself Hope wasn't watching me, judging me, hating me because I was here and she wasn't. Mia was sketching the photograph. In black and white, Hope seemed much less happy. It was as though Mia was painting her ghost, the harsh pencil strokes adding ancient years to her face.

"It's incredible. You're very talented."

Her cheeks reddened like they always did when she was embarrassed by praise. "Mum, how come you never talk about Hope?"

"What? I do. All the time."

She narrowed her eyes. "Not really."

I sat on her bed and interlaced my fingers. "What do you want to know?"

For some unknown, unknowable reason, panic was streaking through my body like a torrent of fire. I made my exterior calm and open and not, I hoped, as strangled and terrified as I felt inside. I smiled and forced myself to look into Mia's eyes and project the message this conversation wasn't making me want to run away as fast as I could.

"I don't know," she said. "Like, did you have a secret language? What sort of games did you used to play? Did you ever play pranks on each other? Stuff like that. I've never had a sister."

"Pranks," I repeated dully.

I rarely let myself reminisce about Hope. Because whenever I did, some awful unfair image would come to me. Like now, I saw myself sneaking up behind her in the kitchen and yanking her dress over her head, and then, when she was screaming and begging me to give it back, I threw it in the bin. "Maybe that'll stop you snooping in my room, bitch." I heard her sobs, and felt her nails rake down my arm before she stormed in her underwear through the house and up the stairs. I remembered feeling like I'd won, like making my little sister cry was a good thing. A victory.

Sisters fight. It's a fact of life. Don't be so hard on yourself.

But was that fighting? Or was that bullying?

"Um, yes, we did." I shook my head and rose to my feet slowly. "I'll tell you about them soon, sweetheart. But I need to take a shower. Mummy stinks to high heaven from all the book talk."

"I'm not a baby. You don't have to call yourself *Mummy*."

I stumbled from the room.

It wasn't fair.

I had countless memories of being loving and kind to Hope.

Liar.

I have countless memories of being a good big sister, I affirmed loudly in my humming mind. And yet my thoughts so often settled on the worst ones, as though even after eighteen years I still deserved to hate myself for what happened.

28

I hated sitting in the dead-quiet office waiting for a phone call that never happened. I sat there, my mind swimming, the buzz from the coffee I'd had fifteen minutes earlier already fading away. Sometimes I read on my Kindle or watched videos on my phone, and other times I closed my eyes and told myself again and again that so many people would be thankful to be getting paid for this.

But I hated it.

With nothing to aim for, my mind played tricks on me. More and more lately, it was returning to Hope, to the evening and the rain and the hill and the car smashing her into broken pieces. Or I'd stress about Troy and his book, wondering if he was going to finish it. Or, if he did finish it, if the publisher would change their mind last minute and not take it. Or Russ: school, stamping down his spirit, stealing his childlike enthusiasm for the simple things.

Mother hated me. Father didn't see me anymore, not really. I might well have Cecelia's madness inside of me, waiting to jump out.

This was all counterproductive, but I supposed that was the

essence of anxiety. It didn't matter that Russ was doing better since Troy had started working from home. He seemed happy to have his father there to drop him off and pick him up from school. October half term had been a godsend too, with Troy and Russ making dens in the house and their laughter filling me with relief every time I crossed the threshold. It didn't matter my family was stabilising again, Russ hadn't wet the bed recently, I'd had another payday and it had been as ego-boosting as the last.

Sitting here in the hazy lamplight of the office, all I could do was pray for the incessant pounding of my heartbeat to quieten down for a minute, just one goddamned minute.

Since my income was what we were relying upon now, I didn't dare show any sign of my stress. Despite my promise to myself, it had most definitely become an Unsaid Thing. Troy was a good man, an amazing husband; if he knew how badly this job was screwing with my head, he'd make me cut down my hours or quit altogether. I didn't want that. I liked having him rely on me, trust me, as I'd relied on and trusted him for the past decade. I wanted to be the strong one for once. I didn't want to fail. We were a team.

So I always dressed as impeccably as I could. I held myself upright and dignified. I adopted the steely ice of Mother, handling myself with poise, and when I felt the mania coming, I directed it toward work. I bullied clients and Clive clapped me on the back for it. I defeated Derrick and Zora's snide remarks by pretending they were insects buzzing around the office, the tiniest of nuisances. I painted my face until I looked like somebody else.

Even Mother had commented on how well I seemed to be doing lately. "You're like a brand-new person, Grace," she'd said over coffee a few days earlier. "You used to seem so childlike, in a sense, so trapped in the minutia of raising your children. A noble endeavour, of course, don't mistake me. But you seem so strong."

"Thank you, Mother."

Thank you, Mother, for loving the mask I'm wearing more than you ever loved me.

Still, it was something; it was more than she'd ever dished out before. I was working hard and earning good money and my family was happy. I was paying for my children's school uniforms and hobbies. I had a husband who loved me and who I loved. I was living as close to the dream as it was possible to get. I wished my whirring thoughts would slow down long enough for me to enjoy it.

Soon, I decided, I'd quit coffee. I knew it was the caffeine messing me up. Some people didn't do well on it. I'd read about it. Panic attacks, anxiety, insomnia. I knew all of this. And yet I didn't feel as if I could stop, which was pathetic, really. There were support groups for alcohol and drug and cigarette addiction, but coffee?

I turned back to my Kindle, trying to lose myself in the light and airy romance Margaret had selected for this month's read. Thank God. I didn't think I could handle another hard-hitting story about death and sisterhood.

The phone rang.

I jolted and dropped the Kindle on my desk, and I stared at the phone as though it was a figment of my mind. I had really begun to believe it would never ring. I quickly picked up the receiver.

"Hello?" a growly voice said before I could speak. "Are you there? Are you listening?"

A tingle scraped over my skin. Already I knew this was wrong. This wasn't how this was supposed to go at all.

"Yes, hello? You've come through to the offices of Langdale Consulting—"

"Pfft," the man grunted. "Listen to you. Pretending. Pretending you're normal. Pretending you're not evil. Pretending it's not all your fault."

"I think you might have the wrong number."

"I don't think so." He laughed harshly. "It's all your fault. And you know it is. You can lie to your family and your friends and anybody else you fucking want, but you can't lie to me."

"This isn't very funny." My voice trembled. "What are you, some bored pathetic teenager? Ringing people up and trying to scare them? Well, it's not going to work."

"I know what you did." He laughed grimly. "And one day so will everybody else."

"I don't know who you think you are but you need to shut the fuck up before I ring the—"

"Goodnight, Grace."

Grace.

"How do you know my name? How do you know my fucking name?"

The line went dead.

29

I stumbled through the office and down the stairs, bashing the door open with my shoulder and pacing onto the street. I grabbed my hips and forced myself to suck in the bracing autumn air, letting it flow coolly around my body.

Whoever it was, I told myself, it was just a stupid prank call. They knew my name, fine, but how hard would that be to find out?

I was on the website. Perhaps they knew I was working late. Perhaps they were a friend of Clive's and this was their idea of a joke. Perhaps it was the client and this was why I'd been waiting here all along, as some sort of sick sexual thing. This was what excited him, scaring women, making them panic and causing their minds to catapult into the past. If it was the client, of course he'd know my name. That didn't explain what he'd said though.

Was he talking about that evening? I'd heard the phrase so many times. In my own head. Aimed at myself.

It's all your fault.

Was it true? He'd said he was going to tell everybody, but tell them what?

I felt a whiplash in my mind, a near-physical tremor rioting through me and roaring not to go there, never to go there, leave it alone, leave it locked, locked tight, Pandora's fucking Box, ignore it, *ignore it.*

Forever.

I walked toward Queen's Square and then turned back, pacing up and down the street, struggling to get my breathing under control. Was he talking about the hill and the car and the rain and my little sister? But why, why the fuck would some stranger do that?

Unless he wasn't a stranger.

Unless Clive was behind it somehow.

Unless Clive had it out for me for some reason.

I told myself to get it together. A prank call, that was it, and I couldn't afford for it to be anything else. I'd need to talk to Clive about it, tell him I couldn't do this overtime anymore. We had crazy sadistic people ringing up trying to mess with my mental health and it wasn't fair. I thought about ringing my best friend, Yasmin, and venting to her. I knew she'd listen for as long as I needed. But my mobile was upstairs and by the time I returned to the office – switching on every light I passed – an evil thought had slipped into my mind.

It was stupid. Of course it was stupid. I wasn't crazy and that was why it was stupid.

I was living in a constant state of unreality caused by lack of sleep, a shimmering film over everything, my nerves pulled so tightly it was only a matter of days or weeks before they snapped. I wasn't crazy, but the thought gnawing at the edge of my reason didn't go away.

Did that phone call really happen?

I collapsed into my chair and stared at the phone and willed it to ring again, to convince myself it was real, it'd happened.

In my research about insomnia, I'd read about people having

far more vivid hallucinations than a growly voice over a crackly telephone. But if I had imagined it, that begged the question of why the hell I would do that to myself. I wasn't guilty of Hope riding down the hill. I was there, fine. Perhaps I should've taken better care of her. But guilty? Did I push her? *No, no, no.* So it wasn't fair to say I was guilty, for my mind to conjure up a phantom voice in the night and—

I stopped, hearing the flow of my thoughts and letting out a mirthless laugh.

I picked up the telephone and hit redial, but of course the sad loser had withheld their details. Fine. Whatever. Some freak wanted to ring up and say cruel things, probably touching himself at the same time, doing some weird fetish stuff like tying a noose around his neck as he choked himself to climax.

A noose and a gouge across her throat for good measure.

"Fine," I snapped, glaring at the phone. "See if I care, you sad fucking freak."

I took out my mobile and opened my and Clive's text thread. *Just had a prank call and the man knew my name,* I typed. *I don't appreciate this, Clive. If it was the client, this is completely out of order. Please ask IT to find out who did this and tell them to stop. Or, I'm sorry, I won't be able to do this kind of overtime anymore. I don't care how important this client thinks he is.*

My finger hovered over Send. I hesitated, staring at the message. I couldn't afford to be this blunt with Clive, not when I was still in my probationary period, and definitely not when I was the sole breadwinner in the household. And, and... I didn't want to think this, to entertain a notion so absurd. But what if IT came back and told me we'd received no phone calls that night?

What if I *had* imagined it?

It was ridiculous.

Of course I hadn't dreamt up a voice.

It was a prank caller.

I wasn't my grandmother.

I wasn't mad.

It was a prank fucking caller.

I deleted the message, and then I picked up my Kindle and read until my eyes ached and it was time to go home.

30

"It's only a small advance," Troy was saying, more passion in his voice than he'd ever displayed at my parents' dining table before. It was a few days after the phone call and I'd battered it to the rear of my mind. I would ignore it. Forever. I was good at that. Very good. I hardly ever thought about the man in the black hat anymore, except in my dreams. "But it's the start of something. I can feel it. It's going to be published on a quicker timescale than traditional publishing, which works great for me. I get to write, really write, for my job. What do I care if I have to work hard if the work doesn't feel like work?"

Work, work, work, please say it one more time, honey.

It was an unfair thought. Troy had every right to be pleased.

I made myself smile as I looked across the table at him, wearing a smart blue shirt buttoned all the way up. He dressed like we were going to church when we came to my childhood home. Hope was watching, as always, with her six judgemental eyes. I felt them searing into me and I ignored them.

"We're so proud of you, Grace," Father said, offering me what seemed like a genuine smile. Nicholas was buttoned up too, with a green sweater and a shirt underneath. The only sad thing about him was the resigned pain in his eyes. "It's so modern."

"What's modern about a woman pulling her finger out and getting on with it, dear?" Mother said. "We've been doing that from time immemorial."

I bit down another unfair sentiment. Mother was grandstanding about women working when she'd never had to work a day in her life after marriage. She'd tried to be a writer for a little while and then Father had supported her with his successful CFO position. I'd gain nothing from expressing how I truly felt. I had to be unbreakable. I had to be pristine and untouchable and outwardly happy. Otherwise it all might come tumbling out.

What, though? What was *all*? A few reports and a prank phone call? A stranger in a baseball cap?

Get it together, Gracie.

We finished our meals and then Father and Russ went into his workshop. Troy and Mia were in the living room, watching some fantasy film as Mia sketched quietly, and I found Mother in the kitchen, pouring a rather large glass of wine. She raised her eyebrow at me and I nodded, and she silently took down a glass and poured me a generous helping. It was these moments – a subtle look, a subtle nod – that made me long for the days before the hit-and-run, when we didn't have all this shared guilt and blame simmering between us.

We went to the kitchen bar. We sat and sipped and stared out at the night-dark garden for a time.

"Mother."

"Yes?"

"How much do you know about what happened to your mother? Cecilia?"

I felt the tension move through her. "Why?"

"I'm just curious," I lied. "I was wondering how it starts. Is it little things, or did she wake up one day and start seeing things that weren't there? Is it induced by stress? Does it have anything to do with caffeine intake? Does it have anything to do with insomnia?"

Mother regarded me coolly. Her eyes took on a glassy quality, as though part of her was receding from the conversation. I imagined she'd mentally skipped across the garden to her office, sinking into her armchair, safe and warm in the embrace of her classics. "Isn't this what the internet is for?"

"I suppose. But I was... never mind. It doesn't matter."

"Are you feeling okay? In yourself? You're not... are you?"

"No, Mother," I snapped. "I'm not going mad."

She recoiled. "I never said that. Or anything even remotely like that. Please don't put words in my mouth."

"Fine, I'm sorry." I felt about twelve. "Excuse me for trying to have a conversation with my own mother."

She stared at me. And then she spoke in a voice barely above a whisper, turning to the night. "I didn't see the beginning. I don't know if she started hearing voices on the wind or started to lose sleep, if it was a gradual transformation, or if one day this evil illness struck and changed her in a heartbeat."

"It's treated differently these days—"

"I know," Mother said tartly. "How is that supposed to help me? Yes, if she had been born decades later, perhaps she would have received the help she needed. Perhaps she would have flourished. But she wasn't. She didn't. I don't know how it started for her. All I know is where she ended up, swinging on a rope with blood streaking down her naked body. That was where my mother ended up. There, Grace, are you happy now? Is that what you wanted to hear?"

"No." I grabbed my glass of wine and took a long sip. I slammed it down and stared at her. She seemed so small, so vulnerable. "I'm sorry that happened to you. I'm sorry I brought it up. I'm sorry, Mother."

Her eyes widened a fraction. She knew I was talking about more than this conversation. She tipped her chin up, stiffened her features, retreating quickly from any emotional closeness with me. "Well, there's certainly no need to get dramatic. And of course you will talk to somebody if you ever feel... like that, like my mother. Won't you, Grace?"

"Of course. But like I said, I'm fine."

"Well then. Right. Excellent."

"Excellent," I echoed.

I went to take another sip of wine and then realised I was empty. Mother saw and smiled tightly, and then with an illicit sort of shrug – as though we were debutantes playing hooky from a ball – she slid her glass across the bar toward me. I wished I could capture this moment, this tiny morsel, and extend it for hours and hours. I wanted to throw my arms around her and beg for help. But of course that would have been rather uncouth of me, so I took a greedy gulp of her wine instead. That was much more civilised.

31

A few nights later, I was sitting in the living room nursing a large glass of red wine, which I'd taken to drinking as a sort of anaesthetic. When I drank enough, I didn't have to think about... well, I didn't have to think about *anything*. I knew this was a dangerous thing to be toying with, and I was careful to not drink too much. But the temptation of complete and utter oblivion was perilously real.

This was my first glass that evening. I'd only had a couple of sips when I heard the sound of my daughter crying from upstairs. She was raging, stamping her feet.

I leapt up, forgetting the wine, and ran up the stairs. Troy was already standing at her bedroom door.

"Mia," I said, my eyes moving over the scene.

All her sketches and her paintings – the ones she'd been sticking to her walls since she was a toddler – lay in crumpled paper petals on her bedroom floor. She had tears in her eyes and her fists were bunched.

"Why have you torn down all your lovely paintings?" My voice cracked, my emotions far too close to the surface.

It's your fault.

Mia slumped onto the bed and folded her arms, toeing the floor. I heard Russ moving around in his bedroom, probably waking at the sound of the commotion.

"Mia?"

It's all your fault.

She looked up and then my phone blared from my pocket. Troy looked at me, face tight, and I knew he was giving me a silent message to answer it. More and more lately, Clive had been ringing me after working hours. It was always with some bothersome task for me to complete on my work laptop. The look my husband gave me said, *I know it's a pain in the arse, but you're the breadwinner now, and it has to be done.*

I took out my mobile. Of course it was Clive. But when I answered, he hung up. Fine, screw him. I needed to help my daughter.

"Mia, your paintings. What happened?"

Again my phone rang, blaring loudly, as if purposefully interrupting me.

"It's okay," Troy said. "I'll talk to her. What do you think, Mia? Want to have a chat with your old man?"

"I don't care."

The sight of Mia like this, usually so composed and now anything but, caused tears to rise in my eyes.

I made to answer my phone again. It went dead.

A moment later, a text came through from Clive: *Signal is terrible. I need you to pick up a work-related package. They know you're coming. I'll text you the address. This is IMPORTANT, Grace. I'm sorry for any inconvenience.*

A stabbing sensation lanced through my skull. Clive was taking the fucking biscuit. He'd already pushed far past any reasonable limits, and this was getting thoroughly ridiculous. Not only was I the hand-copier of useless reports. Not only was I the warden of a phone that only dickheads who wanted to play sick games with me rang. Now I was his courier.

I looked at Troy and Mia, sitting side by side on the bed. Troy was in his dressing gown and Mia was in her grey pyjamas, looking smart with her buttons done up all the way to the top, except for her hair, all mussed and tangled. Her eyes were red, and Troy took off his dressing gown and draped it over our daughter's shoulders.

I have to do it for them.

If I didn't go, I could be fired. Any moment the scythe could drop.

"I'm going into work. I won't be long. Okay, Mia? I won't be long."

Mia sniffled and Troy hugged her close to him. Even if it was unfair of me, I couldn't help but feel jealous at the sight. I turned toward the bedroom, imagining what it would be like to scratch my fingernails down Clive's face, to slash him hard and deep so he bled and never stopped bleeding. He had it out for me. He was torturing me, playing macabre games with me, the same way my grandfather had played games with Cecilia.

But why?

What had I ever done to Clive?

32

I was in Gold Street, one of the more crime-ridden streets in Bristol. It was the sort of area the adults in our lives had always warned us to avoid. After Hope's death I'd spent a fair amount of time around here, smoking, drinking, generally doing what I shouldn't be doing because it was easier than trying to deal with what had happened.

I felt out of place, dressed in my blazer and my trousers with my heels clicking far too loudly on the stone pathway.

As I walked from my car toward the cluster of houses – dance music pumping from the one I was heading for – a group of teenagers in tracksuits asked to borrow my phone. They needed to make a call, they claimed. It was important. His mum was sick. I kept my head down and walked quicker.

"Stuck-up slut," they called after me.

Perhaps it was prejudicial. Perhaps it made me a bad person. Perhaps I was exactly what was wrong with modern England and blah-blah-blah, but it was clear to me, as I stood there trying to summon the courage to knock on the door, this was a drug dealer's residence.

My employer had sent me to pick up drugs.

A light rain fell and settled coolly on the back of my neck. I stood up straighter and made myself Work Grace, which was essentially Mother. I'd do this and then get the hell out of here. I should have walked away. I was an idiot for not doing so. But the sleeplessness and the anxiety and the catastrophising told me if I left now, I'd lose my job, and if I lost my job I'd fail my family. And I couldn't fail my family, not when Troy had worked so hard for so many years at a job he hated.

The doorbell was broken. I hammered with my fist so they'd hear me past the music.

"All right, all right," somebody grumbled from the other side. "Who the fuck is it?"

"I'm here on behalf of Clive Langdale."

"Ooh-err." The man laughed. "You sound like you're here on behalf of the queen."

A round of laughter went up and rage pricked me. "I'm here to collect a package. I haven't got all night. I'd be grateful if you'd hurry up."

The door swung open and a tall shirtless man stepped forward. His torso was a patchwork of tattoos and when he smiled, the swollen roll-up between his teeth bobbed suggestively. "No need to get excited, sweetheart. I was just having a laugh."

"Yes, well," I muttered non-committally.

"You're not the usual type we get here. Your name ain't Grace by any chance, is it? We've been expecting you."

I bristled. The last thing I wanted was these men knowing my name. The smell of marijuana came blasting from the house. I breathed as shallowly as I could. I'd experienced the high – or low – at university and had no desire to repeat it. I remembered the paranoia, the screaming at the edge of my reality, the way the floor seemed to swerve toward the ceiling as I knelt next to the toilet, panting.

It's not my fault, it's not my fault, I'd ranted, as my flatmates giggled and exchanged looks of hilarity, one of them asking what wasn't my fault. "She's a lightweight. She'll be all right in a minute." I couldn't tell them; I didn't know. I *couldn't* know. Yasmin was rubbing my back and yelling at them to get the fuck away from me, and then asking me quietly afterward what I was talking about. It was the first time I told the story of that evening, half-remembered through a haze of intoxication and shame.

"Do you have the package?" I asked, snapping back to the present.

"Ain't even Christmas and you're getting a proper sweet bundle. Yeah, wait here. Unless you wanna come in for a drink?"

"I'll wait here."

"Suit yourself."

I tried to project the appearance of a strong controlled person as I stood there. Even as my heartbeat tried to choke me out, I made myself stiff. I clasped my hands behind my back. But when the man brought out the package and I saw what it was, I felt my chest seize and my hands flutter in panic. "What sort of game is this?"

He laughed. "Spunky, ain't you? Listen, darling. I don't know why your bloke wanted me to wrap up this fine product like this. But I'm not about to hold a goddamn inquiry on the doorstep about it. Are you taking it or not?"

Don't take it.

Before I had a chance to answer, he thrust the package into my hands and slammed the door in my face. I stared down at it, my mouth dry, wondering how my life had led me here, to this moment, collecting what could only be drugs for a client of Clive's. But the worst part was how it was presented: wrapped in green wrapping paper, with small white trees dotted all over it, tied with a red ribbon.

It was the same wrapping paper we'd used on Hope's final Christmas.

I took out the plastic bag I'd stowed in my pocket and shoved the package inside, wondering why Clive was doing this. Or perhaps Mother was behind this somehow; she'd observed her father first-hand and learnt his methods, and she was exacting her long-awaited punishment. She hated me.

This was proof. Somebody was out to get me.

But it could also be true this was an inside joke between these drug dealers and Clive's client. But he'd said he didn't know why *my bloke* had wanted it wrapped like this. Who was this bloke?

I shoved the bag into the footwell of the passenger side and gripped the steering wheel, gripped it until my knuckles became skeletal. I had to glance at the package several times to convince myself it was real.

My mind skirted close to the possibility Clive was *him*, the bonnet in the rain, slicing—

But whenever my thoughts steered too close to that evening – to anything after she started pedalling – I felt a gnawing at the fabric of something unknowable. It was as though something was trying to break through. And I wouldn't let it. The bottom of that hill would forever remain dark.

I picked up the bag and ran my hands over the wrapping paper. Hope had giggled so sweetly when she'd torn open her present to find the doll inside, complete with a miniature vanity unit and a hairbrush. She'd spent hours and hours arranging everything, brushing its hair.

She wouldn't let me near it. She was afraid I'd break it in front of her just to hurt her, to see her cry, because that was me, the wicked older sister, the vindictive sadistic bitch—

Quiet, Grace.

I searched my mind and tried to remember if this was, in

fact, the exact same wrapping paper. Or if it was close. Or perhaps it was utterly different and it was nothing to do with me; I was only a pawn in Clive's bizarre approach to business. I was out of my depth and floundering.

It was driving me insane.

I cursed quietly and threw the package down, and then drove through the night toward the Langdale Consulting offices. I thought about opening it, and told myself I didn't because a client's trust mattered too much to me; it had nothing to do with the notion of tearing the paper away to reveal severed fingers and reeking eyeballs and a braid of brown hair turned bristly with time.

I stowed the package under Clive's desk and drove home. Soon I'd have to make a stand. I'd have it out with Clive and figure out what was going on. I couldn't live like this. It wasn't fair. I needed one good night's sleep. Just one. Then I'd be able to think all of this through with something approaching clarity. As it was, I was a blind woman in a mist-covered field, no idea how far I'd gone or how far I had to go.

When I returned home, I wore my smiling, everything-is-okay face. But I prayed for Troy to sense something was wrong. I sat down at the kitchen table and took the proffered hot chocolate, and I silently willed him to see how badly I was losing it.

"How's Mia?" I asked.

"Sleeping. One of the kids at school made a joke about her being a crap artist. She took it to heart. You know how she is. Anyway, we had a talk. I think she needed to vent. I wish she wouldn't keep everything locked inside her so much sometimes, you know?"

We're similar in that way.

"Yes. I do know."

"She's put most of the pictures back up. She decided not to let immature dickheads dictate her life."

"I hope those weren't her words."

Troy wrapped his hand around mine which was curled around my mug, enveloping me in warmth from all angles. "I was thinking we could have a little shindig for your birthday. What do you think? We'll have to invite my parents, which'll be a pain in the arse. But it could be fun. We'll do our own thing too, a meal, a hotel room, maybe a chariot ride."

"A chariot ride?" I laughed hollowly. "Aren't you pushing the boat out? Yeah, that sounds nice. I'll invite Yasmin. And maybe Olivia from work."

He smiled and I smiled and inside I was dying a little, but my husband didn't notice. Or he didn't want to notice.

It's him. He's behind all of this, a voice hissed. *Don't trust him. You can't trust anyone.*

33

"I don't see why I can't meet this client. I know what you're going to say. You're going to tell me this is an unorthodox company, a hipster company, whatever. You do things your own way. Fine. But not even being able to meet the man I was sent to pick up drugs for is ridiculous, Clive."

Clive's face dropped and he peered at the door behind me, double-checking it was closed. He fiddled with his Rolex and let out a sigh that made his jowls tremble. "Jesus, will you keep your fucking voice down? I don't think the deaf bloke in Cornwall heard you."

"Don't you agree?" I strode up to his desk. "I don't remember you mentioning any of this in the interview. Copying those reports by hand, fine, perhaps that's a quirk. But the phone calls, waiting for the phone calls that never come?"

"Never?" Clive asked, perking up a little.

It's all your fault.

"Never. And picking up drugs? I've committed a criminal offence for you and if you think that is in any way acceptable, I'm fucking done."

"Grace, it was a bloody bootleg games console for my nephew. I knew this bloke who knew this bloke who got some cheap. They wrapped it up as a joke. When I spoke to him about it I asked if they did a wrapping service. I'm sorry I lied, all right? Jesus."

"A games console." He was lying to my face, he was lying… but why? Why? It wasn't my fault. "So why did you tell me it was for a client?"

"Because he was gonna sell it to somebody else and I didn't know who to send. They're all right. Maybe they smoke a joint every now and then. But so what? Did you think I'd sent you to pick up a big bag of cocaine or something?"

"Well—"

He sat forward, becoming the Clive he was in client meetings, when the feelings of whoever he was talking to were secondary to the objective. He gained a new purpose and suddenly seemed less defensive.

"Grace, you're doing a great job. You're confident as hell, you're bloody smart and you're a quick learner, all right? I value having you on my team. But if you think you're working for the kind of company that would send you to collect a package of drugs, then you're in the wrong place. The report copying assignments are for a – like you said – a man with character quirks. The phone calls are an inconvenience, but fucking hell, getting paid to sit next to a phone and play Solitaire for an evening? You've got a habit of looking gift horses in the mouth and if you honestly don't think you can trust me, then you know what to do."

He was looking at me like he hated me, like I was somebody else, some enemy in his life who'd wronged him. I cleared my throat and took a step back. "Are you firing me?"

"Don't be so bloody dramatic. I'm just telling you. Don't start making accusations when you haven't got any evidence. If you really thought you were there to pick up drugs, why did you do it? What sort of person would go through with that?"

"I..."

The sentence that rose on my lips would seem melodramatic, like I was the victim, and I wasn't the victim. *I did it for my family.* He'd laugh in my face. And he'd be right to. I'd picked up what I thought was a package of drugs – risking prison – for my family? It made no sense.

"And the wrapping paper?" I asked after a pause.

"Like I said, it was their idea of a joke—"

"No, I mean the *style* of wrapping paper."

"What do you mean? It was just wrapping paper."

Actually, Clive, I'll have you know it was the same wrapping paper we used on my dead sister's last Christmas with us. I checked on Facebook last night.

What the hell was I thinking? I couldn't say this at work. I couldn't say this anywhere. I couldn't even check; the package was gone.

I turned toward the door. "All right then," I said, as if that meant anything.

I went into my office and kept my head down for the rest of the day, going over and over the package in my head, trying to remember if it could've been a games console. But wasn't it soft? They could have bound it in bubble wrap. But was it heavy enough to be a games console? I couldn't remember.

Perhaps I'd let my mind play a trick on me.

Again.

Like the phone call. When you imagined somebody's voice.

I squeezed the edge of the desk and let out a shivering breath through clenched teeth. My belly stung with last night's wine, guzzled at midnight as my house slept. My eyes ached with lack of sleep and too much staring. My body felt hollowed out, somehow. I didn't want to admit weakness, fine, but was I really supposed to keep all of this bottled up inside?

I'd have to talk to Troy about lowering my hours or even quitting. I'd come too close to falling into my own mind. It was time he knew what I was going through; it was time I shook him awake instead of lying like a dead woman next to him all night, my eyes open, staring lifelessly at the ceiling.

But when I got home, Troy gathered me into the living room. Vanilla-scented candles were lit and flickered along the mantelpiece of the fireplace. Mia was quietly proud and Russ was bubbly as they wrestled over who got to show me the A3 card. Mia had drawn a yawning nature scene, with rivers and hills and, in the sky, a soaring woman with the wind at her back. *World's Most Hardworking Mummy*, the text read, each letter meticulously drawn and painted.

"Time for the best bit." Russie opened the card and pushed it into my hands. "It's eighty-two, Mummy. I counted. Didn't I, Mia? Didn't I count?"

"Yeah." Mia smiled, rolling her eyes. "Out loud. It was really annoying."

"Why eighty-two?" I asked.

"One for every day you've worked at Langdale Consulting," Troy said, massaging my shoulder and leaning over to kiss a warm tear from my cheek.

"Count them, Mummy!"

He leapt into my lap and I felt a sob rise in my throat. My son took my hand and moved my forefinger to each one of his thumbprints. They were every colour of paint Mia owned. Reds and greens and blues and purples, a glorious mess of colours, and in the middle of it all was a smiley face made of thumbprints.

I should have relished the moment, but a cruel feeling settled over me. The smile was all red paint and it looked bloody, like liquid red oozing from broken gums. Troy had encouraged the children to do this today, of all days, when I was especially stressed about work.

I glanced at Troy, still in his dressing gown, worn over pyjama trousers and a baggy T-shirt. He looked so comfortable. Did he know I'd wanted to talk about lowering my hours? Perhaps he'd arranged all this, somehow, so he could work from home forever. Or perhaps he wasn't working. Perhaps he was doing something else. But then I saw his smile and the genuine love in his eyes. I remembered university and the solid way he'd looked at me when I told him I was pregnant. Troy wouldn't manipulate me.

Wouldn't he?

I couldn't quit, regardless. The World's Most Hardworking Mummy didn't throw in the towel when things got rough.

"Eighty-two," Russ yelled, throwing his hands in the air. "Told you."

34

It was a cosy autumn evening and, instead of watching a film with my family or making love to my husband, I was in a dead-quiet office copying meaningless reports for a man I had never met.

I wrote out the words feeling like the world's biggest idiot. Clive was taking advantage. He thought he could bend me over the desk and take me if he wanted. What sort of twisted fetish freaky niche arcane shit was this? The more I wrote the more it felt as if this entire endeavour were designed to convince me I was going mad.

But why, and who? Who? Clive, was Clive the one littering these reports with references to car collisions, rain, slippery roads, and even once an explicit *hit-and-run* metaphor, a bonnet slicing through the rain and a bicycle wheel spinning around and around and—

I slammed my eyes shut and leaned back in the chair, grounding myself, taking shaky breaths and telling myself to get a grip. I had to be strong. Russie and Mia and Troy needed me. I couldn't let Cecilia's genes come out to play. I had to stay here, present.

Heartbeat: hammering.

Breaking my chest and causing big gulping noises to sound at the back of my throat.

I was being foolish, I knew, and soon realised this when I'd managed to get my breathing under control. It was a panic attack, a normal everyday thing, another hazard like needles in the street and knives up dirty alleys and all of life's rotten shit, except it was in my head. It was in my head and it hurt.

I felt like a coiled spring ready to snap open any second.

I couldn't explain this pounding inside of me, as though something buried deep long ago was trying to break the surface. Like there was an oil derrick inside my skull slowly bashing away, but why, for what? All I knew was I couldn't sleep and I felt anxious, but surely that described many people who were beginning a new career. That was what I felt, I decided, I hoped: the usual workplace jitters.

It was a windy night and the office was settling down, which meant it was becoming a creaky tool of paranoia. Each whine through the building became the footsteps of a man who had stumbled in from the street and was here to stab me, charge in here and attack me viciously. Or it was the wind. But it was impossible to know and each time those phantom squeaks came closer, I'd sit back and watch the door like a hunting bird. I'd laugh at myself, as in, *ha-ha, the crazy lady is watching the door.* But I kept watching.

Each time, it was nothing. It wasn't Clive, who for some reason was out to get me. Clive Langdale had a grand plan for me. Clive Langdale wanted to turn me into my grandmother. I knew my thoughts were becoming jumbled. Fine, but it was the truth, because the car crash references, the overtime, the phone call... It was Clive. Clive called me up that night. Clive had been writing the reports. Clive sent me to pick up drugs, despite what lies he'd told me afterward. Why, did he record me?

He had a recording of me collecting drugs and soon he'd use it to blackmail me.

Because he hated me? But why would he hate me?

A jagged thought struck as my mind spiralled, the same thought I'd been trying to ignore for weeks.

He was *him*.

He was the nameless bonnet. He was the rain slashing through the wind. He was the stupid beautiful novelty bike and the unreliable English weather.

Clive had killed Hope and tracked me down and he was using the job to torture me and drive me as mad as my grandmother...

Why, why the fuck would he do that? Even if he'd killed her, and that was nothing more than a sick thought, but even then this made no sense. It was too motiveless. Surely he'd just be happy to get away with it. But then what if there was another reason? Did I know Clive from university?

Shut the fuck up, Grace, I told myself, and forced my eyes to focus on the computer screen. Mr Big needed his reports doing and I wasn't about to die on this hill. Fine, let my paranoia flare, but this job was supporting my family, and that meant more to me than any false claim on sanity. If my job had to drive me slightly mad to make it bearable, then I would only join the ranks of the majority who felt the same way. Nobody liked work, except Troy's brother, Keith, the wildlife photographer.

And Troy now, I reflected warmly.

There.

That was reason enough to stiffen my upper lip and carry on.

But then I heard a creaking noise from the Pen.

It was nothing. It was the wind. There wasn't a killer or a thief or a devil out there. I was already laughing at myself when the quality of the noise changed. It went from the *reeeeeek* of a persistent wind to the unmistakable pitter-patter of footsteps.

They padded by outside the door and then the handle turned, slowly, as though the person was unsure of whether or not they were allowed to enter. It turned and turned and then cracked open a sliver and my breath caught in my throat like I'd been stabbed.

An arm came around the edge of the door, hazy in the light of the corner lamps.

The arm was a little girl's and she was wearing a bracelet. There were little clinking seashells and rocks on it. It was the bracelet that hung in Father's workshop. Except it was here now. It was Hope's and it was here.

The door swung open and from the deeper darkness of the office the little girl stepped inside.

She looked at me uncertainly, this beautiful girl, this perfect girl. She had braided brown hair and she was wearing the same summery dress Hope had been wearing when she died.

There were rabbits on the dress.

There had been rabbits on Hope's dress that evening.

I can't breathe. Why can't I breathe?

As she took a shaky step into the office, her bracelet clattered quietly as it always did.

"You can never lose Hope, can you?" Father had often said, smiling as she swaggered around the kitchen, shaking her wrist proudly. Hope had danced and twirled into the garden and the bracelet sang like a shell-bird.

She gazed at me, clearly shaken and distressed from wherever she'd been.

"Who are you?" I asked, only the voice wasn't my own.

I was speaking with a dead woman's voice.

"H-Hope," the girl said shakily.

I screamed.

132

35

The girl spun and darted away from me. Her braid trailed behind her the way Hope's had, whipping around the edge of the door as she skipped from the room.

My throat tore from screaming, and cruelly I saw myself yanking on her braid once when we were arguing, losing my temper, the sort of horrible memory that was supposed to die with your loved one. I'd yanked her around the edge of the door and she'd let out a puppyish scream, and I'd felt *happy* about it.

"W-wait," I gasped.

She pitter-pattered across the floor.

I struggled to my feet, everything feeling sensitive, as though my skin was suddenly sunburnt. Hyperreal, the world speared at me. Any moment somebody was going to leap out and attack me.

Somebody knew about my sister.

They were baiting me with her double.

They would kidnap me when I went to see what the hell was going on. They'd sell me at a slave auction and I'd be abused in the most gruesome ways.

I stood at the threshold, these thoughts biting into me as I listened to a door open and then the steps were gone. I moved back. I should've chased her and demanded to know who'd put her up to this.

But what if...

No, it was stupid.

But what if it had been Hope?

Of course not, obviously not, there was some explanation, some angle, but I couldn't think and as I stumbled and held myself against the wall I wondered if maybe it was Hope, my little Hope, and she was back and she'd tell everybody what sort of a sister I really was—

No, no, no, I whimpered in my mind, my voice cut off with a stranglehold of panic. I wouldn't let my mind veer to nasty places, to trick me and make me even more panicked. It was Derrick or Zora, the sneering double act, or it was Clive, or it was Mother, horrible dear Mother who might enjoy watching me squirm at the sight of a well-made doppelganger. It could have been anybody, because everybody had something on me, some gripe, and maybe that was motivation enough to dress a little girl up like my sister and—

It could have been her.

I tried to focus on dragging my breathing back to something like normal. In the end I had to settle for a mutated version of calm. I withdrew inward and turned myself into a zombie. I stared at the wall, waiting for my pulse to stop shimmering and my heart to stop hurting in my chest.

Time passed and eventually I could sleepwalk to the desk, sitting down and letting my head fall back.

It hadn't been Hope.

Somebody had hired a little girl to imitate her because they were out to get me. The light had been hazy. I didn't see her properly.

Her voice, was her voice the same? I couldn't remember. She'd only spoken her name.

Hope.

She'd said it like it *was* her name. Not like she'd been coached to say it, a behaviour any mother could pick up on, like when Russ had to memorise lines and he couldn't help but puff himself up proudly as he said it. But this girl – *Hope, Hope* – she'd said it like it was her name and had always been.

Had the rabbits been the same?

Feed the rabbits. Hope's impression one day, munching on a carrot, Mother gleefully impressed with her youngest daughter's recitation of this famous line.

Feed the rabbits; feed the worms.

Dead now; that wasn't Hope.

Or that was Hope.

Hope had needed to see me. Even if we'd had our differences, she knew I was her big sister and I'd always protect her no matter what. She could've chosen to visit Mother and Father, but for all their fawning they weren't her sister. That meant something, despite what Mother might like to pretend. This was evidence she loved me more. She'd come to visit me and not them.

I laughed at the thought, forcing a grin at the notion of ghosts and ghouls and dead sisters. This wasn't one of Troy's fantasy stories. It was a girl, a flesh-and-blood girl, and somebody had sent her here.

But there was a part of my mind that felt as if it was cracking, or rather that an existing crack was being levered open in violent jerking motions. This part of my mind was focused on the little girl, my dead sister, staring at me and telling me her name. I wondered if she was waiting for me; if I went into the hallway, she'd be standing in the shadows.

"Where are you going?" she'd say. "Don't leave me, sister."

Then she'd leap at me like something feral and clamp her hand on my shoulder, dragging me down and gnawing a bloody chunk from my face.

"Get it together, get it together," I said, achingly aware I sounded like a madwoman.

36

All around me there was laughter and good cheer. It was my birthday party. It was a happy occasion.

Yasmin and my father were talking earnestly. There was something endearing about seeing my tattooed university friend talking with my father about model boats. Troy's dad was holding court, a big chunky man with a thick neck and thick arms who had worked hard labour since he was fourteen. He had a way of dominating the room, and I could see the crow's feet at the edges of Troy's eyes wincing in silent discomfort as he listened. Troy hated it when his father talked about manual labour; it was another slight in their varied catalogue, to be filed alongside, *I hear Keith might be up for an award soon.*

Mother and Phoebe, Troy's mum, were sat on the sofa talking about hair extensions, my mother bringing her hand to her chest. "Good heavens, I don't know if I'd feel comfortable wearing another woman's hair."

"Yeah, but trust me, you'd look well lush with a few pink frilly extensions."

Mother smiled and laughed and I was reminded she was a good person. "You do talk some nonsense, Phoebe."

Phoebe laughed. "Guilty as charged."

I stood in the corner, standing over Mia and Russ and Yasmin's son, Elliot. Russ was explaining that to save Elliot they'd have to electrocute him. "See." He was grinning, holding up two paper clips as though they were defibrillators. "Just one good zap."

Mia, arms folded, sat on the edge of the sofa with one earphone hanging out, looking so intelligent and grown-up, looking like somebody I could imagine going to Paris with one day, if she wasn't too embarrassed, perhaps when she was forty and I was sixty and we'd walk around, the best of friends. "Yeah, sure, that'll work."

I took out my phone again, even if I'd promised myself I wouldn't this evening. I couldn't bear it. But I stared down at the screen, because it was doing something very strange. It had been doing this very strange thing ever since Hope visited me the previous night.

Almost every time I looked at my phone, there it was, there *she* was.

A note was open and text was writing itself, typing across the screen. I brought it to my face and tried to breathe quietly as people spoke all around me, and the music played, and Russ laughed and Elliot mock-groaned as he was electrocuted.

Why did you scream? the text read. *Do you still feel guilty? Do you think I want to hurt you like you hurt me?*

I love you, I love you, I love you.

I shivered and felt tears prick my eyes, but somehow I maintained a look of calm.

"Gracie?" Troy laughed, finally breaking off from the sermon with George. "Hello? Earth to Grace?"

I turned the phone to him to show him the message. I somehow did it without letting out a sob. I expected him to ask me why I'd written it to myself. *Had* I written it to myself without realising, all these times?

He smiled a little shakily, as though he was trying to work out if I was telling an unfunny joke. "An empty memo, spooky. Have you still not worked out how to use that thing? What was it, a meme?"

I looked at the screen. The note was empty.

It's him. It's your husband. He typed the message and now he's deleted it, and he's laughing at you. He's secretly laughing at you. He's sneering behind those kind eyes, that's what he does, he works against you and makes sick private jokes and watches as he drives you mad.

Because...

Oh, no.

Because Troy was the one who killed Hope, and that's why he'd sought me out at the university party. Troy was the one behind the job and the little girl and the text, somehow, he'd what—cast a spell, cast a spell on my phone.

Listen to yourself, Grace, listen to yourself.

I laughed, masking whatever was happening inside of me. I made myself smile radiantly. I was having a fun birthday party and nobody could prove otherwise. "I've had a little too much to drink. But you know what? I might get a little more."

I walked into the kitchen, as bright as I could be, and found Olivia leaning against the counter talking with Yasmin. I flinched at the sight of Yasmin. Hadn't she just been talking with Father? But it was possible I'd been staring at the text longer than I'd thought. Time did bizarre things when it ran on no sleep.

Olivia was laughing and nodding and I gestured at the fridge, which was between them.

"Look at Gracie." Yasmin giggled, giving me a look that threw me back a decade. "Are you going wild tonight then? I don't blame you. If I'm not absolutely smashed on my birthday, I consider myself a complete failure."

I cracked open a cider and blackcurrant and took a sip from the can. "Maybe a tad. What were you two talking about?"

I sipped.

Was it me? Were you talking about me?

"About Olivia's new man, this proper disgustingly handsome hunk she's been screwing for a few months."

"We were *not*." Olivia glared, and I wondered if it was a lie, a joke to hide the fact they'd been discussing how funny it was my husband had killed my sister and was playing a sick mind game on me.

Shut the fuck up, Grace.

"Really?" Yasmin laughed. "I guess somebody slipped me some LSD then, because I seem to remember you bragging about him being burly *and* bookish, which seems like an impossible combination to me."

Olivia gazed, face tight, as though she didn't want to talk about this in front of me. Why? What was she hiding? What was she thinking?

"Thanks for coming though, guys," I said, after a pause.

"When you said it was on you, I was in," Olivia said, in a hiding-something voice. "Nah, I'm joking. Happy birthday."

We walked over to the window that looked out upon the garden, at the trampoline. I gestured with my cider can, and tried not to think about the text and the little girl, the little girl with the bracelet and Hope's braided brown hair. She'd been wearing Hope's dress, and—

And I wouldn't think about that. "I built that thing, you know."

"Really?" Yasmin asked. "How absolutely modern of you."

"Yes, I'm a great example of the modern woman. Strong, unbreakable, that's me."

"Hey." Yasmin wrapped her arm around my shoulder and gave me a short hug. "You are, you know. I'm always telling people how you went from being a stay-at-home mum to the breadwinner. It's great."

I nodded and yet a part of me was thinking about those long adventurous afternoons with Russ, sitting on the beach with one eye on the Kindle and one eye on him, with the sky grey and the wind whipping bracingly. It wasn't all fun. There was duty there, and that felt good; it felt good to see my son build a castle and fail and then convince him to build it again. It felt good to hug him as he cried and tell him everything was going to be okay.

I wished I could climb into those memories, secreted away in unceasing bliss, where spinning bike wheels and impossible girl ghosts and unapproachable guilt could never hurt me.

37

I stumbled into the living room and sat down and drank the cider. It was my first cider, but my fourth drink of the party and my sixth of the day. Red wine was still bubbling in my belly.

You're drunk. You imagined the text. None of what happened was your fault.

Nobody could creep into my mind and twist my reason, play psychopathic tricks on me, make me see messages that weren't there and girls that weren't there and anything that wasn't there. I knew what reality was, for Christ's sake. I could trust my senses, my memory, my mind. I'd work out who was doing this and why.

After a few minutes I realised somebody was talking to me, *at* me, some acquaintance. I was taking deeper and deeper breaths, but quietly, my own silent terrified moment. I felt as if I'd floated up and out of my body, and I was looking down at her, at me, and seeing how small and weak and vulnerable we looked. I took a large, large sip of my cider and then there was no cider left.

It was then I heard my husband's voice, raised in a high, half-posh way, affected as a defence mechanism, a very particular sound I associated with him arguing with his father. I looked across the room and saw Troy's cheeks tremble and his skin bloom red. "Well, I don't see it—"

"Most men," George cut in, "they want to be the earners in the household. I know you've got your own little arrangement going on here. But when do you reckon you'll be earning again, proper like?"

"I am earning," Troy said, sounding like a boy.

I hated it, hated that I couldn't trust Troy or anybody and that my thoughts never settled, as though I was stuck in a loop, a sleepless endless loop that would eventually tie a knot around my neck. I hated that Troy couldn't stand up to his father and I hated George for making him feel as though he had to.

"It works quite well, actually." My voice rang out icy cold across the room. I did not sound like I felt. I sounded strong. I sounded deadly. I sounded like somebody who didn't have to be scared all the time, so let's have it, if he truly wanted it, let's have the big mess out in the open. I was rising to my feet and striding forward and all the time moving like nothing could stop me. "We don't see it as an issue of husband and wife or man and woman. We see ourselves as partners. Troy supported my dream of staying home with the children and now I'm supporting his of becoming a writer. I don't see that just because Troy was born with a dick and a pair of bollocks it should make any difference. Why do you always have to fucking put him down, George?"

All the energy drained from the room and even if the music kept playing, it seemed quieter somehow. George didn't get angry or even furrow his eyebrows. He smiled like I was joking and then looked at Troy as if to say, *What are you going to do, lad? Your wench is starting up.*

"Why are you looking at him?" I hissed.

"Listen, darling," he said. "I didn't mean to upset you, all right?"

"No, I really want to know," I persisted, even as Troy put a hand on my arm and asked me to calm down. "Don't tell me to calm down." I lashed his hand away and turned back to George. "I wasn't asking for the sake of it. Why do you have to make him feel fucking worthless?"

"Grace." It was Troy. "The kids."

But I could barely hear him, so important had this moment become. Alcohol and caffeine and anxiety swirled through me. Perhaps if I could fix this for Troy, it would make everything okay. I wouldn't have to worry about the text and the phone call and the drugs and the present, the man in the black hat...

How had I been so stupid? How did I not understand this was more than Clive's business? Somebody was out to get me. Somebody was coming to get me and on the phone, the prank caller, it had been a *man's* voice. It could be George. It could be Troy's dad because he wanted to wound Troy for disappointing him as a son, he was using me to get to him, he was somehow sending the texts and had arranged for the girl—the girl with Hope's bracelet...

"Father?" I said suddenly, looking around the room for him.

I felt George looking at Troy again. I had snapped, in an instant, from the argument to this thought.

"Um, yes?" Father frowned. He did not like confrontation.

It was him, it was him.

"Hope's bracelet, the one that hangs in your workshop, has it been stolen recently?"

"No, it was in there this morning. Why?"

"But somebody could remake it."

"What do you mean?"

The whole room was watching and I noticed several people who seemed to believe they were looking at a madwoman, when really I was trying to puzzle this out. Olivia's face was narrow and severe, and she looked like she might cry, which made no sense, and then she turned and walked out without saying a word. Her mother. I vaguely remembered her mother was ill. What was it? Dementia, a sickness of memory. I understood that. It was me. It was my fault.

Focus, Grace.

"The r-rocks," I said, hating that I stuttered. "And the shells. Somebody could find some rocks and shells and drill holes in them if they wanted to remake it."

"I suppose so," Father muttered.

"They couldn't," Mother interjected. "Of course they couldn't remake her bracelet. It's one of a kind. It's utterly unique."

"Mother, I didn't mean—"

"It's as individual as a snowflake, with all those special quirks she applied. She was always so, well, hopeful, wasn't she? Of course her bracelet couldn't be *remade*."

"No, of course not."

It's your fault. It's your fault. You killed her.

I turned to George, but I'd forgotten why I'd been so angry with him. It all seemed so meaningless. I looked around the room and saw Russ with tears in his eyes and Mia staring at me in concern.

When Mia saw me look her way, my sweet daughter strode across the room and placed her hand in mine. She was so real. "Mum, come see my painting. You'll really like it. It's one I did last night when you were at work."

I gratefully followed my daughter out, feeling a river of love flow between us as we walked up the stairs and into my bedroom. I sat on the end of the bed and she sat on the vanity mirror chair, so I could see the back of her head in triplicate. She had such beautiful well-behaved hair.

"Did you have too much to drink, Mum?"

"You shouldn't be talking about things like that."

"I was around Kelly's house one time and her mum drank too much."

"Kelly?"

Mia frowned. "You know Kelly. I met her at the after-school art class. I've went around her house for dinner like five times."

"I don't remember…"

I felt tears spring to my eyes as I frantically scoured my mind for any mention of this girl Kelly, but there was nothing, no conversation, no fragment. My mind was filled with the desire for real sleep and the demons, the horrible long list of them.

There was something cruel about not knowing the name of my daughter's friend. There was something wrong with me.

"I'm a terrible mother."

"What?" Mia laughed quietly. "Okay, yeah, you're the worst mum in the world."

"I really am."

"Mum, come on, you're actually making me want to be sick."

I smiled and felt a single teardrop slide down my cheek. "Is that right?"

"Yeah." She shot me a mega-pout. "You really are. Go to sleep and you'll feel better tomorrow. That's what you and Dad always tell us."

Go to sleep, ha-fucking-ha.

"Yeah, that's a good idea. I love you, Mia. You know that, don't you? The day you were born was the happiest day of my life."

"You always say that."

"Because it's true."

"Okay, goodnight, Mum."

She walked from the room and I threw myself backward, too numb to climb under the duvet. I curled my knees to my chest and lay there, listening to Troy and George downstairs. George's voice was raised and he sounded so reasonable, so understanding. "I don't know what I said to upset her."

I wrapped a pillow around my head and tried to block out the voices. But they were still there, jeering through the material. I buried my face in the blackness of the pillow and screamed long and hard until my throat hurt.

This was enough. This was too much. I couldn't do this anymore. It had to stop.

38

The next morning – feeling like a husk hunched over my desk, in no state to be at work – I tried to convince myself everything was okay. I wasn't spinning like a bicycle wheel out of control and I wouldn't roll out of my life and lose any sense of what I was. I wasn't snapping, cracking, anything.

I was normal. I was Grace Dixon. I was regular and middle-class and I went on camping holidays and drank lattes and there was no way I was splintered down the middle, a broken piece of chinaware.

I stared at my computer screen and knew I couldn't do any work. With the party and the girl – *my sister* – weighing me down I couldn't focus; focus came and went but mostly went. Troy had smoothed things over with George, but this morning he'd looked at me like I was my grandmother, as though he could already see a jagged red line across my throat.

"I think we need to talk later, Gracie." He rubbed my shoulder kindly.

About how you're driving me insane? a bitter mad voice whispered.

The text—the faceless man in the black hat—the phone call —the girl—the Christmas present...

I buried my face in my hands and made a quivering trapped sound.

When a knock pounded at the door, I leapt up and let out a cry.

I clamped my hand over my mouth and killed the noise, taking a wheezing breath through my fingers. I wished I could sleep, lay on the desk and close my eyes and drift into nothingness. My body buzzed. Olivia hadn't brought me a coffee yet, and I didn't want to leave the sanctuary of my office to get one myself.

"Yes?" I snapped, far angrier than was justified.

"It's me," Derrick said, sounding inconvenienced like he always did.

"Fine."

He opened the door and walked over to my desk and said something about a report. But it was the look in his eye that spoke louder than any words. It was as though he could see through my clothes and he was enjoying it, this petty power over me. He wore his perpetual smirk and I knew it was him, the sick bastard, the one who'd sent Hope. He thought I was sleeping with Clive and so had arranged for my little sister to come and visit me.

Fuck you, Derrick.

It made no sense. None of this made sense. No sleep since the party. No sleep in who-knew-how-long. I was sneering at him, and I was nodding and making hmm noises as though what he was saying – whatever it was – was the most important thing I'd ever heard.

"But then you think I'm a whore anyway," I broke in.

He paused. "What?"

"You think I'm a slut. You think I fucked Clive to get this job.

You and Zora probably call me a whore and all manner of names behind my back. That's your opinion of me, isn't it, Derrick? I have a feeling something happened to you to make you hate women, especially promiscuous women, which you seem to believe I am for some reason."

He glanced at the open office door and the noise beyond, as if it offered safety. Then he smiled tightly and shook his head. "I don't know where this is coming from—"

"From your clumsy hints. From your little jabs. You know where it's coming from but you're not used to women defending themselves. So here's an idea. Get the fuck away from me and get it into your thick fucking skull I would never, in a billion years, do anything sexual with Clive. Okay? Fine? *Fuck off.*"

Derrick backed out, hands raised, a man who'd suddenly realised he was in a cage with a lion and not a house cat. I reeled and sat, panting, and Derrick must've said something because a few minutes later Olivia poked her head around my office door. "Grace? Is everything okay?"

"Sure. I was just thinking about getting a coffee. Do you want one?"

She winced. She looked like she was in pain, somehow, for some reason. "Maybe you should go easy on the coffees." She walked toward my desk. The door swung closed behind her, sealing us in together. "I think you need to calm down a little."

"Calm down?" I laughed. "Why? I'm fine. I drank too much last night. It happens to the best of us."

"You don't need any more coffees." There were tears in her eyes as she gazed at me, her lower lip trembling. "I'm so sorry."

"Sorry? Sorry for what?"

She turned and her face fell. "Nothing."

"No," I snarled, standing up and pacing around the desk. I grabbed her arm and gazed at her firmly. I felt like I could break her arm if I wanted to. I made her look at me. "What the fuck do you mean, you're sorry? Why would you be sorry?"

"I didn't think you'd get this bad." Her words were contorted with her sobbing. "I didn't mean to... I didn't want to..."

I grabbed her shoulders and shoved her right up against the wall. As I leaned close and growled in her face, it felt right. I was cracking. Fine. Fuck it. Then let me shatter. "What are you talking about?"

"The coffees," she whimpered, cringing away from my hands. Guilt streaked her features. It made her look younger, like Mia on the rare occasions she didn't do the right thing. "I shouldn't have... I didn't want to—"

"What did you do?" I screamed, part of me wondering if this was a dream. "Olivia, tell me what you did."

"I've been spiking your coffees. I've been drugging you this entire time."

I'm awake. I'm asleep.

"Why?"

"He made me. I'm sorry. I didn't want to. But he made me."

"Who made you?

I'm awake I'm asleep I'm awake I'm—

She lightly brushed my hands away, as though I was a clinging branch in the woods, a mild inconvenience. She strode to the desk and she let out a shaky sigh. And then she told me.

39

The reports, the package, the late nights, the drugged coffees, Hope, dear little Hope, it all led here. Olivia had told me his name was Sonny Hatton, but that meant nothing to me. Perhaps it was a fake name, or perhaps somebody had hired this Sonny.

Mother hired him. Troy hired him. Clive hired him. The whole world is conspiring against you. Walk. Get out of the car and walk.

I felt like a zombie as I climbed from the car and dragged myself toward the house, a semi-detached in Weston-super-Mare. The walls were white but coloured with wind and time and sand. There was a child's bicycle in the front garden, one of the wheels missing, upside down and laying on the rain-damp grass.

Of course it had to be a bike; it was a sign.

This is real, I told myself firmly, feeling the coastal breeze shiver over me. *This is not a dream.*

"He made me do it," Olivia had whimpered. "I didn't want to. I wish I hadn't."

"You've been drugging me since the start."

"Yes."

I knocked and felt the reverberation go up my arm.

Footsteps sounded behind the door, getting closer. As I was wondering how long it would take for me to turn and sprint to the car, he emerged.

"Oh." I gasped. "It's you."

"Grace," the man said. "I think you should come inside."

"No." I took a step back. "Tell me what you did. What did you make *her* do? What did you put in my coffee? Why are you doing this to me?"

He frowned. "You really have no idea?"

I think I might. But I never look there. I never let myself.

"No."

"Come inside and we'll talk about it."

"Tell me here."

He made to grab my wrist and I snapped, lashing my hand up and striking him across the face. He took the blow, a feral look creeping into his eyes. "Don't do that again," he warned.

"Or what?" I yelled, raising my hand again. "Tell me what the fuck is going on!"

"Grace, please keep your voice down."

He made to grab my wrist again, and again I moved back, aiming a slap at his face. He slid aside, easily dodging the blow. He was still frowning.

I don't want to do this, his eyes said, even as he did it.

He moved with the speed of a predator, whipping his fist and smacking me across the jaw. I felt my brain wobble in my skull and then I was falling.

As the world suddenly turned to night, he caught me and dragged me inside.

40

I woke with a heavy feeling in my body, as though invisible weights were dragging me down.

My wrists were sticky and when I tugged on them, something strained. I pulled harder and then sat back, feeling the duct tape over my mouth and the wooden chair beneath me. My hands were tied too, wrapped with layers of tape.

I was in a cellar.

Dust coated the floor and the walls and I struggled to suck in air through my nose. My face pounded from where he'd hit me, a headache making a tight band of tension around my forehead.

With a creak that went right into my centre, the door at the top of the stairs opened and he walked slowly down, his figure a dim silhouette in the hazy bulb light.

"It's time to face the truth, Grace."

I writhed and tried to scream, but the tape kept my lips tightly shut. The chair leapt up and down; that was as far as my protest could go. My heart thumped in the back of my neck and threatened to choke me.

"You know what I'm talking about," he said. "I pushed her."

Fucking no. Please God, no.

I strained against the bindings with everything I had. A slight smirk touched his lips and he stepped closer.

"I pushed her down the hill. I mean, I made her go, I called her names. I'm always calling her names."

Stop, stop, stop, stop.

He knelt and laid his elbows on his knees, tilting his head at me like we were old friends. "I said she was a baby. And she wouldn't do it. And she did. She did."

He was reciting my own words to me.

I couldn't stop it anymore.

The cracks within exploded and shrapnel tore through my mind.

I didn't want to, but I remembered.

I remembered it all.

41

Mother had told me to take Hope out on her new bike and I hated her for it: both of them, Mother for making me do it and Hope for being so smiley all the damn time.

I hated being lumbered with my little sister. I hated having to listen to her cheery voice, and most of all I hated the way Will's face changed when he saw I'd brought a seven-year-old with me. Will was a rugby player, two years older than me, one of the coolest kids in school.

"Why is she here?" He nodded at Hope, who was lingering a few feet away near the fence.

Will and I were standing near the swings. Three ciders sat on the ground, the fourth plastic ring empty from where he'd presumably already drunk one. His hair was swept to the side, an ashy blond, and his pale blue eyes regarded me coolly.

"I invited *you*, Grace," he said, an annoyed note in his voice.

"I know. I didn't want to bring her. Jesus. She's so annoying."

He leaned down to his bag, grabbed the ciders, and quickly zipped them away. "Listen, I've gotta go. Try'n ditch the kid next time."

He walked out of the park. My teenage world upended as I

realised I wouldn't be able to brag to my friends about getting with Will Yard. I'd already told them I was meeting him, so it would be doubly embarrassing. Maybe he was already telling his friends how lame I was, bringing my annoying little sister, about how he'd wanted to drink and maybe smoke and maybe do other things, exciting grown-up things.

She'd ruined it. Hope. I hated her. She was so *annoying.*

"Can we go home now?" she whined, leaning on her stupid pink bike, the ugliest bike I'd ever seen. "Please, Grace?"

I marched past her and we began the long walk home. As if that evening was not already a nightmare, the weather inexplicably changed and the sky darkened. Rain pelted down, soaking me through, drenching my hair.

Why won't she stop smiling?

"You're such a baby," I spat, when we were near the top of Clifton Hill, the first words I'd spoken to her the entire walk home.

"You're just angry that fat boy doesn't want to kiss you."

"He's not fat. He's got muscles. He's a rugby player."

"I bet he already has a girlfriend."

"Shut up. You're a stupid baby. Everyone says you are. Even Mum and Dad say you're a stupid ugly baby."

Her upper lip stiffened and even in the rain I could see tears were budding in her eyes. "You're so mean."

"Going to cry, baby?" I laughed sharply. "Going to cry and ride your little fucking baby bike home? Well? Are you?"

"I'm not a baby."

I laughed again, low and mean. "Sure, sure. You're not an immature little girl at all. When's the last time you kissed a boy?"

"I don't even *want* to do that."

"Nobody will ever want to kiss a skinny bitch like you. I bet you're going to be flat-chested when you grow up."

"You're so horrible sometimes! And I'm not a baby. I'm more

mature than you. All you want to do is go to parks and kiss boys."

"Kiss?" I yelled, trying to sound haughty. "God, is that what you think boys and girls do? You really are pathetic."

Perhaps the way her cheeks trembled was giving me some sort of pleasure. Perhaps the pain in her voice lessened the blow of what I imagined Will was doing. Telling his friends. Making me a laughing stock.

She looked at the ground and let out a choking noise. For a moment I felt something, a pang of regret, and I saw myself going to her and placing my hand on her shoulder. I saw myself squeezing her supportively and telling her how sorry I was, I'd never be this cruel to her again, I loved her.

But then I remembered Will's face, the way his eyes had glinted in mockery and disappointment.

"You're the baby," she huffed, as we crested the hill.

"Yeah?" I sneered. "If you're not a baby, ride down that hill."

"What?"

"If you're such a big girl, ride down that hill, as fast as you can. Or are you scared?"

"I'm not scared."

"So you'll do it?" I goaded, knowing she wouldn't, knowing I'd win, whatever the hell winning meant in these circumstances. "You'll ride down the hill as fast as you can to prove you're not a snivelling pathetic ugly baby?"

"It's too wet—"

"That sounds like something a baby would say."

"Another time—"

"You know you can't do it."

"Another time. It's raining."

"How cute, the skinny bitch is *scared*."

"I'm not scared!" she screamed, tightening her grip on the

handlebars and spinning the bike around in one fluid motion. "And I'm not a baby. You're the baby!"

"Go on," I taunted, walking over to her. "As if you're going to do it. I'd do it, if I had my bike. I've done it before, actually, loads of times."

Hope peered down the hill. A few strands of her auburn hair had come loose, spiralling. "Really?"

"Yep," I lied. "It's easy, even in the rain. For big girls anyway. Not for little—"

Hope climbed onto her bike and I was still smirking at her, secure in the knowledge she would step off the bike and bow her head and this argument would be mine, mine in that evil teenage-girl way that meant nothing. It meant I'd wounded my little sister again, tore down another brick of her self-esteem. And for what? Because Will fucking Yard wouldn't be plying me with cider and stuffing his clammy hand down my knickers tonight.

"You're really going to do it, are you?" I cackled. "Yeah right."

"You'll see."

To my utter disbelief, she ducked her head and pedalled toward the lip of the hill. Her braid fluttered behind her and my voice broke in a scream, my primal instinct rising above my bully's pride.

"Hope, stop. Hope, fucking *stop*."

But it was too late. Hope was a stubborn girl. She was the sort of girl who'd search for hours for the perfect rock at Weston-super-Mare, skipping over the stones like a wraith.

I chased her, panting, tripping more than once. Everything was soaked. My throat was hoarse with screaming and I kept thinking, *Please be okay, please be okay.* I promised myself I'd never bully her again if she was okay. I'd always be a good older sister. I'd protect her like Mother and Father were always impressing upon me.

Let her be okay.

But of course she wasn't. She was seven and it was raining and the hill was steep and what she'd done was reckless, stupid, and not her fault. No piece of the blame was hers. It all belonged to me.

42

"I used to joyride my dad's car around the South West," the man said, but I was hardly listening. I was in an abyss of memory, all my fears stacked up, attacking me. "I liked to grip the steering wheel hard. I'd imagine I could feel every little bump in the road. I'd speed around roundabouts and my heartbeat, Grace, it would go mental."

He looked at me expectantly. The duct tape burned against my lips. My tears burned hotter.

Hope, little hope, and it was me.

It was always you, the hateful voice inside of me hissed.

"Normally my dad would be working the night shift at the supermarket when I took the car out. He walked because it was close and the car wasn't insured, wasn't even in our name in any sense of the word."

He nodded, as though proud. I worked my wrists in the duct tape. I was sweaty. It wasn't very tight. Maybe there was a way out of this bastard's trap.

Or maybe I'd die here. Like Hope died. Like I killed her.

"Sometimes I'd go right up to Clifton. I'd drive to the edge and stare down at the River Avon. I don't remember what I was thinking that evening. I try to bring it back, what was going through my head when I was sitting there smoking." He paused and took the cigarette from behind his ear, lighting it and inhaling deeply. "I don't remember what I was thinking the last time I was innocent. Something's wrong with that."

He paused and stared and smoked for a few minutes, and I was forced to sit there, wondering if he'd leap across the room and do vicious things to me.

The memory hadn't been real. Deep down, I'd known something was twisted with me and my sister. I knew I resented the clicking seashells on her bracelet and her seaside smile.

I was a teenage girl, cruel, as we sometimes are.

"You remember how quickly the weather changed," the man said. "Started pissing down in seconds."

Of course I remembered. It was typical English weather. *Rain, rain, go away*, Hope had sung once, tapping her fingernails against the bedroom window, and I'd had to fight the urge to grip her hair and smear her face against the glass.

What was wrong with me?

"I didn't feel like I was over the speed limit, but then, fuck, this blur jumped out. She crashed against the bonnet and went slapping over the roof and onto the tarmac behind me, a twisted thing lying in a red puddle."

The image blared loudly, the red of a comic book or a graphic novel, one of those over-stylised films Troy liked. And yet it was also hazy, appearing and vanishing, as though my mind's defences weren't ready to quit.

"I threw the car door open. I felt like I was going to pass out as I walked toward her. I looked down and she wasn't moving. There was nothing I could do. She was broken."

He stared and smoked, one hand tucked in his pocket. I eyed the way his fingers shifted around in there. Did he have a weapon? He could slit my throat any time the notion popped into his deranged mind.

"Here's the funny thing." He exhaled a grey cloud of smoke. "Well, not funny. Odd. I've heard you mention her bike wheel was spinning. I've heard you say that quite a few times. But it wasn't spinning. The bike was destroyed. I've thought about that, and I think you invented the bike wheel so you wouldn't have to remember how messed up her body looked."

I couldn't refute his words. I felt raw and used-up, gnarled from all those sleepless nights and all the stress. I didn't understand my memory, my*self*, because anything I consulted may turn out to be another lie. Madness had finally caught up with me.

He was silent for a long time. Finally he flicked the butt to the floor.

It was a dusty cellar, with a washing machine on one end and a wicker basket filled with shoes and boots opposite. There were more items, the detritus of life, but it was the shape of the room that interested me.

He was on one side of the rectangle and I was on the other. If he remained over there, he wouldn't see me wriggling my wrist, working at the duct tape.

"I stood there for a long time," he said. "I guess I was waiting for one of the house doors to open... for somebody to shout at me and tell me to stay there so they could call the police. But nobody came.

"Then *you* came running down the hill, a thirteen-year-old girl with tangled wet hair and mud all up your arms, your top all coated in muck, your jeans dirty. I think you were crying, but it was raining too much to see.

"You were choking and gulping between your words. You told me you'd pushed her and I asked you what you meant."

I could feel the words on my lips, through the duct tape, the admission I'd given to this stranger. The root of my madness had been planted there. My mind splintered and a fiction took the place of reality.

"None of it seemed real. You know what I mean."

Of course I knew what he meant.

"You told me you'd talked her into cycling down the hill. You'd called her names and bullied her."

I pushed her, the teenage version of me croaked in my mind. *I called her names. I'm always calling her names. I said she was a baby and she wouldn't do it and she did, she did.*

Mother was right about me.

"You kept moaning you'd killed your little sister. You asked me if she'd be alive if you hadn't forced her down the hill. Maybe it was cruel, the answer I gave you. I said yes. She would be alive."

I let out a sob, muffled by the tape, the same noise I'd made that evening. I remembered the sensation of it in my throat, and then I forced it away.

"I didn't want to go to prison. You'd given me a way out. You begged me, Grace."

I'd cried and sobbed, pleading with him not to tell my parents. Mother had made me promise to take care of Hope. Father had smiled at me, standing in the front window, his hand raised with the suggestion of a tremor. He was concerned I couldn't do it. But I could; I'd prove I could.

Or kill her, ha-ha-ha, the mad thing inside of me cheered. *The little bitch deserved it, right, Gracie?*

"If you'd been calm I wouldn't have been able to slowly back toward my car. If you'd been older you would've known you shouldn't let me drive away. I called over to you before getting in. Do you remember yet?"

I remembered, and it fucking hurt.

If you tell anyone you saw me, I'll tell your parents the truth. I'll tell them you killed your sister.

"I got into the car quickly. I didn't want to see the effect my words had on you."

He'd driven off before I'd collapsed atop her, my hands in her soaked matted hair, crying for relief.

43

"When I got home I drove the car down the side alley. It was overgrown and covered in grass, and soon I was driving in mulchy mud. I stopped near the rusty barbeque our neighbours had abandoned, killed the engine, and let out a long breath. It made a shuddering sound and I realised I was crying. I'd been crying the whole way home."

He was relentless, pacing up and down the cellar, waving his hands as he spoke. It was like he was possessed, and telling this story was the only way to exorcise the demon. He clawed at his pocket and withdrew a cigarette, lighting it efficiently.

I stared, playing the patient captive as I worked at the duct tape with small movements. I was reeling from all he'd told me, from all I'd remembered – appearing and disappearing like a drowning woman on the ocean's surface – but Mia, Troy and Russ were waiting for me.

"I went inside and sat at the kitchen table, the one we got at the charity shop, with a few scuffs here and there, only sixty-five quid for the whole set, including the chairs. It was a bargain."

His eyes shone with reminiscence. For a deranged moment, I felt myself smiling beneath the tape. I corrected the gesture.

"My dad was working the night shift, so I sat there. I sat and hugged myself. I was so scared, but I knew I could never tell anybody, not so they'd understand. I was as broken as that little girl."

He shuddered as he inhaled a long plume. I turned my face away, unwilling to gaze upon the sadness. It reminded me too much of my own.

"Finally, Dad came home. It was morning. The sun was rising in the kitchen. He asked me what was wrong when he found me paralysed at that charity-shop table. 'The car's out back. There's blood on the bonnet. I think I'm going to prison.'

"He kept asking for more detail, but I couldn't talk anymore. I was crying again. This was before I learned how to be cold, I guess, because I was blubbering like a little kid."

There was real pain in his voice, or at least real-*sounding* pain. He worked his jaws from side to side. I got the sense he was sharing only a tenth of his thoughts: much of this was passing through him silently, as painfully as it had worked its way through me over the years.

"Eventually Dad left to look at the car." He flicked the half-smoked cigarette away and stuffed his hands in his pockets. "When he came back, his face told me the rain hadn't cleaned everything off. There was blood all over the bonnet and—fuck, I'm sorry, Grace. What's wrong with me?"

He turned and frowned, and our eyes met. Terror flared in me... Did he know what I was doing with my hands?

But it wasn't only fear of capture that made me want to scream. It was the pity I felt at his expression, as though I'd done this to him, hurt him in this evil way. And I had; I'd talked Hope into her death dive.

But it wasn't fucking fair.

He'd knocked me out and tied me to a chair. He was a monster. He didn't deserve my empathy.

"'You fled the scene,' my dad told me, and let me tell you, Martin Evans could put some real meanness into his voice. He grabbed the back of my neck and shoved me against the table, crushing my cheek. He started calling me names: sicko, freak, stuff like that, venting his anger and pushing me harder and harder against the table. I didn't have the energy to fight. All I could do was tell him he was hurting me, and my voice came out wheezy."

He became Russ for a moment, his voice shivering and afraid. My maternal instinct awoke, but I couldn't allow myself to care about this man's plight. He was my enemy. Shared experience didn't change that.

"Dad started talking to himself, sort of muttering," he went on, tucking yet another cigarette behind his ear. The room was thick and musty with the stench of smoke. "He talked about how the car wasn't taxed or insured and how nobody knew we had it, except a few people around the estate, and they'd rather die than talk to the police. He had a friend who worked on a scrapheap. Dad wouldn't look at me, but he'd help me get away with murder.

"'Take those clothes off,' he told me. 'Go upstairs and have a shower. Go into work tomorrow with a smile on your face like you're one of the fucking gang. Act normal.'

"I tried to tell him I didn't know if I could act normal, and he jumped at me. Martin was a big man and, if it weren't for his supermarket uniform, you'd think he worked as a labourer or in a warehouse or something. Plus, I knew he'd boxed when he was young.

"He told me I didn't have a choice. What was I going to say? He was my dad and he knew best. I didn't want to go to prison, Grace."

He stared as though he thought I could speak, forgetting

he'd cut off my words. His eyes brimmed with a desire for forgiveness; I recognised the look from the mirror.

"I took off my hoodie and my T-shirt and my trackie bottoms. And then my boxers and my socks. I'd already taken my trainers off when I came in, because habits are funny like that, I guess, so I nodded to where they were. I stood there naked, covering my privates.

"Dad told me to go upstairs. He was already lifting his mobile to his ear, one of those big chunky Nokias, you remember them. I called out to him. I started to tell him I was sorry, but he walked out and shut the door."

He laughed bitterly, without humour. "My own fucking dad didn't look at me. I don't think he could."

44

The man walked over to the washing machine and leaned against it, crossing his arms. "I guess none of this really matters, does it? There's nothing we can do to change the past."

He turned, his eyes flitting over me. He wouldn't look directly, as though he couldn't bear to face the fact he'd tied a woman to a chair. Guilt dripped from him. He had the look of a man on the verge of asking me how he could help, if only he could forget he was the one who'd put me here.

"But I've never talked about this before. I want to."

He kicked away from the washing machine, resuming his relentless pacing.

"Dad said I had to go on as normal, so that morning, I went to work. I wasn't in any state to. I couldn't stop thinking about that poor little girl. But I made myself be friendly with my manager and flirty with this girl I liked. I had the usual banter with the swimming instructor. I was working as a lifeguard.

"The whole time, I was wondering if I was a killer. Maybe she wasn't dead, I was telling myself. Maybe she was... And see, Grace, there's the fucking problem. Maybe she's what? The chances of her being fine were pretty much zero. I knew that."

She wasn't fine. She was shattered and I'd pawed at her, trying to put her back together like Humpty Dumpty.

"Time kept passing. A month, two. I read the newspapers and found out what I already knew. The girl was dead. The story was prominent for a while, but it didn't get national attention.

"That seemed weird. It had all the ingredients for a story the big newspapers would love. A pretty little girl hit while riding a bike she'd got for her birthday... How could the press *not* eat that shit up?

"I think it was how your parents came across in the police appeals. They were sort of nothingy, if that makes sense. Some parents, they get the public going because people can speculate if they were involved. Or they tug at their heartstrings. *Something*, you know. But your parents didn't cry. They spoke like they weren't even there. They gave the public nothing to get worked up about."

He hadn't seen how Mother and Father had privately devastated each other, with their coldness and their detachment, with their retreating into the past; he hadn't seen Father secluded in his workshop, captivated by Hope's bracelet, wishing he was back there, in the day she made it. He hadn't seen Mother sunken into her armchair, submerged in a novel she'd read dozens of times, determined to live anywhere but reality.

"I thought about you a lot, as time went on. I hated you."

The feeling's mutual, dickhead, I snapped silently. I'd have given five years of my life to have the duct tape removed. To scream would've been such a relief.

"I don't have any siblings, but it didn't make sense to me that you'd do that. I don't mean to make you feel bad. I know you've tortured yourself about this over the years. But it really disgusted me, how irresponsible you'd been. How cruel to your own flesh and blood."

The question was too huge for me to contemplate. Some form of sickness had led me to bully sweet Hope, a resentment I couldn't comprehend.

"I learnt your names. Grace and Hope Addington. They seemed like really fancy names. I read you hadn't seen anything, hadn't seen anybody. Apparently, your sister had decided to ride down the rainy hill herself. It was a horrible accident and nothing more. I read all of this over the weeks and months. And then your story went away.

"But I remembered your names. I remembered the photos that appeared in the newspaper. They even printed the name of your street, not directly, but they quoted one of your neighbours. It was one of those bigger pieces, hit-and-run, what did this mean for the local neighbourhood? That sort of thing."

That was probably around the time I'd haunted Hope's grave most afternoons, telling myself I'd hear her voice on the wind one day, calling to me: when my mind began to bend around my perception of myself, editing out anything that didn't fit, rewriting whole sisterhoods.

"I hated myself. Hope was so cute. So beautiful. She had such a nice smile, didn't she? At least from what I saw in the photos. She reminded me of a puppy, an innocent puppy, and I'd killed her. I'd ended everything she might've done or been."

I hated him – I wanted to hate him – but it was like he was picking phrases from my mind.

I'd killed her. *I'd* ended everything she might've done or been: a scientist or a champion skier or a fashion designer or anything she wanted to be.

"One evening," he went on, "my dad walked up to my bed in the middle of the night. He stood there stinking of booze, and he had a newspaper crumpled in his hands. He was crying. It was like the day my mum ran out and left us. She took my dog, Rocket. I'll always miss Rocket.

"'Benny,' my old man sobbed, and then he kept asking me why. *Why, why, why.*

"'I'm sorry,' I said, and I sat up.

"'That poor family,' he moaned, sounding like an animal, all strangled and choking."

He'd given me his name, perhaps by accident. *Benny.* I wondered if it was his real name, or another fake one, another lie. He smiled in the awkward way men sometimes do, as though his emotions were so powerful he had to smile or else he'd burst into fitful tears.

"I told him I was sorry again. Then his eyes got glassy and he jumped on me. He punched me in the face. He kept punching."

45

I stilled my hands when Benny strode across the room. He moved with purpose, with violent intent in his posture. I cringed back and prayed he wouldn't be able to see how I'd worried at the duct tape. It was a pathetic effort, perhaps, but it was the only thing keeping me sane.

A voice giggled inside of me, Hope's voice, gnarled with her murder. *Sane, sane, go away. Come again another day.*

"Are you going to scream if I take that off?" He gestured at my face.

I shook my head, ashamed by my trembling. It was like there was a busted fuse inside of me and it wouldn't stop sparking.

"I'm not going to hurt you, Grace." He tore off the duct tape. I gasped as it stung my skin. "Sorry. It's better to get it over with."

"Water, please." I purposefully made my voice polite. I was a survivor. Fuck this self-pitying *shit*. I'd have to make him think I liked him... or, at least, I didn't hate him. Which I *did*, didn't I? I had to hate him.

"Sure." He got a bottle from behind the washing machine, tossing it from hand to hand as he carried it over. "Do you want me to help?"

I laughed bitterly, my voice raspy. "I can't exactly take it, can I?"

He was behaving as though we were having brunch or something, overly casual, overly *friendly*. He was forgetting he'd told me a fake name; he'd lied to me every moment we were together.

"Well, Benny? What are you waiting for?"

I glared at him. For a mad moment – *every moment for you then, he-he-he* – I thought I'd tear my hands loose and brutalise him right there.

He unscrewed the lid and brought it to my mouth. "Fair enough."

I drank greedily, lapping it up.

He took the bottle away, stepping back as he replaced the lid. "I guess you're wondering why I'm telling you all this."

"No. I understand."

"Do you?" he asked, eyes narrowed.

I made myself breathe slowly, thinking past my pulsing rage. He wanted us to be best bloody pals. It was like he'd separated reality into two lanes: the real one, and the one he wished it was.

I didn't pity him. I didn't like him. I didn't want to make his pain go away.

It was your fault, a mad voice sung: the voice I'd battered down every moment of my life. *It was all your fault.*

"You need to make the memories real." My voice was somehow steady. "I studied memory in university. We make memories real by repeating them."

"How does that work?"

"I don't know. It was a long time ago. I didn't finish university."

"I know."

I sighed. "I guess you know most things about me, Benny, don't you?"

He shook his head, his eyes growing flinty. "Keep it civil, Grace. What were you saying about memories?"

"You create a memory, call it up into your mind," I said, old fragments from textbooks returning to me, but incomplete and hard to make coherent. "So every time you repeat the memory, you make it realer."

"But you can do that by remembering it," Benny said. "You don't have to tell anyone."

"But we don't care about what *we* think of ourselves." I stared at him right in the eyes, thinking of Mia's blurring paintbrush, Russ's half-built sandcastle and Troy sat at his desk, typing away. "All we really care about is how other people think about us."

He chuckled and pulled out his cigarette packet, crunching it into his fist when he saw it was empty. "You think I'm telling you this to make you, what, feel sorry for me?"

"No," I said, unable to mask the feeling in my voice. Did I care, on some instinctive level, about what I'd put this man through? "I think you want somebody to finally know who you really are. I'd like to get to know you."

He swallowed, his throat shifting. "All right, Grace. I'll give you the highlights of the life of Benny bloody Evans. But first you need to tell me something."

"What?"

"Did you believe it, that story you told, about how she'd decided to cycle down the hill on her own?"

I blinked away a tear, nodding.

"How is that possible?" he asked.

"I don't know. I built walls in my mind, I suppose. False memories aren't unheard of. People confess to murders they didn't commit. I was young. I was scared. I was broken."

"How does it feel, remembering?" The corner of his lip was twitching, like he could smirk or grimace any second.

"Horrible," I told him, forcing dignity into my voice as I sat up straighter.

"Yeah," Benny grunted. "I bet it does. All right, let's go on with this."

"My old man kicked the shit out of me. And I mean he *really* kicked the shit out of me."

"That's awful," I whispered.

Meanness crept into his eyes. "Let me get this over with. Then we'll get to the juicy bits, the bits that'll make you pay."

Make me pay? I almost screamed, but I stopped the words at the final moment.

"He got me a dog to say sorry. I told you Mum took our other dog, Rocket, right? Anyway, Dad had never let me have dogs after that. They reminded him of her, I guess. But he brought me this Jack Russell, Boxer. He had a big brown spot over his eye, like an eyepatch, but the rest of him was as white as snow."

There was charisma in his smile. It made me want to smile with him.

"He sounds beautiful."

"He was a rascal. But in the best way. He was so fun. He'd come running with me on the beach, and I'd talk to him about what happened, about how scared I was. I talked to him about how much I hated you, Grace. About how much I blamed you."

I turned my gaze; I didn't trust myself not to snap at him.

"I'm telling you how I felt," he said. "Not how I feel now, necessarily."

I wasn't sure if that made this any better, but I said nothing, obstinately staring elsewhere.

"Anyway, Boxer was my life. The years went on. It's funny how that happens. I remember thinking, *holy shit, it's been ten years since I killed that girl*. And then another five would go by."

"You followed me," I said. "At university."

"And before that."

"Were you the man at Cabot Circus, the one who ran from me? The man in the black hat?"

"Let me tell it my way."

That was no answer, but I could tell he wasn't going to give me anything. He must've been the man in the black hat. What had he spiked my coffees with? Speed, cocaine? Whatever it was, it was turning my mind into a pinball machine. My thoughts sped and crashed into each other.

"I'd driven by your house lots of times over the years," he went on. "I'd sit and watch your old man in there, all fucking hollowed-out, the same way my old man got at the end. I'm getting ahead of myself, dammit. My dad died of lung cancer, Grace. He wouldn't stop smoking. We had an argument about it once, he was coughing up phlegm and still lighting fags, and he lit another right in the middle of the fight. Lit and smoked, and smiled. It was like he wanted to die."

Benny groaned and ran a hand through his hair, pacing quicker, fingers twitching. I wondered if this man could turn violent. But that was the wrong question. He *had* turned violent. I had to make sure he didn't do it again.

"You were watching us," I prompted.

He nodded. "I'd watch your dad mope around. I'd watch you climb out the front window after dark, skipping down the guttering pipe. You moved like a little monkey, Grace. I'd follow you sometimes, and I'd see you in the park, with all those boys passing you around…"

"Fuck off," I hissed. "It wasn't like that. They were my friends."

He held his hands up. "No need to get feisty. The point is, I'd think to myself, *I wish I could save her*. I wish I could make her feel better. Or I'd think the opposite. I'd think about killing you, about how it would feel to punish you for what you'd inflicted on me.

"I checked up on you over the years. I was glad when you found Troy and started a family. I'd seen how much you suffered. I was proud when you went to university. I suppose that's why I waved at you."

So he *was* the man in the black hat. But had he been at Cabot Circus, leading me through town, to those kids who told me nobody had jogged by? Perhaps I'd imagined that part.

I wanted to ask, but I sensed he wouldn't like it.

"I met a woman, Lacy. She's amazing. She's funny and smart and beautiful. She's sassy. I know women hate these words. Lacy does, at least. But what else am I supposed to say? She's the woman of my dreams. We have a kid together, a daughter. She's the best thing that ever happened to me."

"What's her name?"

He scratched at his jaws, covering a smile. "You know, I don't remember."

"You don't remember your daughter's name."

I knew what her damn name was.

"I guess not." He shrugged. "Anyway, Lacy took what we had, this beautiful thing we'd built, and she decided to throw it down the fucking toilet. She had an affair. I found out she was banging this bloke most evenings, telling me she was working on her mobile salon business. She didn't even *have* a business. She made it up so she'd have an alibi for this piece of shit. They were going behind my back for a year, Grace.

"And do you know what she said? I was *cold*. I was *distant*. Of course I bloody was! I'd killed a little girl before I was a man. I couldn't let out one emotion, because then I'd let everything out."

I understood. Sometimes it was better to plug them all.

"It happened so fast. A week after she dropped that bombshell, I had to put Boxer down." He paused, clearing his throat. I couldn't tell if it was from cigarettes or sadness. "He was so brave at the end. His legs were trembling, like he wanted me to take him running on the beach. I think he *was* running, Grace, in those last moments... in his head. Do you believe in that sort of stuff?"

"In heaven?"

"Yeah."

"I don't know."

"No," he said, "neither do I. So Boxer was dead. Lacy was gone. Our daughter was staying with her. But I made damn sure I had all the visitation a man could wish for. I walked her to and from school every day. I had her every other weekend. And sometimes in the week, she'd stay over at mine. Lacy agreed to this because she knew – she *knows* – we're better off as a family."

"I can't imagine the pain of being apart from her."

I could imagine it; I was living it.

"It hurts, that's for damn sure. Then Dad died. The cancer finally got him. This was maybe a month after Boxer. I'd been close to my old man when I was a kid. He taught me to box. That was why I called my dog Boxer. He was such a good, good dog. I know there's something wrong with me, but I miss his happy face and his big smile more than I miss my old man." Benny's voice cracked. He swallowed and went on with a visible effort.

"Anyway, my dad doted on me before I became a killer. He let me get away with murder, no pun intended."

I laughed reflexively, a short puff of air. Benny flinched and let out a short chuckle. Both of us sounded sick, strangled, wrong. The laughter died as soon as it had arisen, confusing and messy.

"He told me he hated me," Benny said. "They were his last words. His biggest regret in life was making my mother pregnant. And then he fucking died."

He stopped pacing, staring at the floor, fists clenched, like Russ on the verge of throwing a tantrum.

"I walked out into the hospital car park, lit a cigarette, looked at the stars and thought about you. You'd made me cold and distant, which is why Lacy left me. You'd made me kill that poor girl, poor innocent Hope, which was why my old man hated me. If Boxer had been alive through this, I don't think we'd be here. That terror-terrier would've saved me."

He glanced at me, lips shivering, tears glistening in his eyes.

"But Boxer was dead. It was time for you to pay."

47

"I followed you." Benny gazed at me. "Sometimes you went to a café to meet with Yasmin. It was easy to sit there and listen to you rant about your life. You're quite a loud speaker and you've got a posh voice. It stands out."

My mind flitted over a thousand café scenes. I'd never considered the strangers surrounding me might have ulterior motives. I should've been more paranoid, like grandmother, questioning everything until there was nothing left but a length of rope and a straight razor.

"I learned you were going to get a job when your son started school. I learned your husband was a writer and you'd had a schizophrenic grandmother, and this really stressed you out. I reckon that's because deep down, Grace, you know your mind is a fucked-up place. So you worried about it more than most people would."

There it was again: his unnerving tendency to pick at my rawest parts. It was as though he'd crawled inside my mind. He was voicing all of my thoughts aloud.

"I got an idea, and I'll admit it was evil. But it was genius too.

It'd help me execute two birds with one beautiful stone. Did I tell you Clive was the bastard Lacy had an affair with?"

"It doesn't surprise me."

"Why do you say that?"

"I work for him," I said. *Eighty-two days*, Russ sang in my mind, willing me to stay strong, to keep gnawing at the duct tape like a stubborn rat. "I've seen him around people. He doesn't respect anyone or anything. It's probably why he's so good at his job."

"She was *wowed* by his suit, his watch and his wallet," Benny grunted. "This wasn't just about you. I was going to make that motherfucker squirm, too. It was all starting to come together."

He looked hard at me, and I wondered if he knew me better than Troy: if eavesdropping on hundreds of conversations ranked over a few serious conversations a year. Perhaps Benny Evans was the person I was closest to, because we shared what nobody else could know.

He stared as if to say, *You know you fucking deserved this.*

Even as I fought it, I knew he was right.

48

"You know about Olivia's mum, don't you, the dementia?"

"Yes."

Benny whistled. "Hell of a thing. She's only sixty. Sometimes Olivia visited her and then went running the second she left. She wore her gear to the visit. She wanted to be ready to get as far away from that place as possible."

I nodded, waiting. He scowled at me, as though he was disappointed in my reaction. I wasn't sure what he wanted. *Praise?*

"We met during one of these runs. It wasn't an accident, obviously. I needed her. I gave her a fake name, like I always do in these situations, picking the first name of one boxer and the surname of another. Sonny Liston and Ricky Hatton, two legends of the sport. Sonny Hatton.

"I was quite aggressive and flirty with her, but she loved it. She was the one who texted me the next day. *Don't keep me waiting.* I saw her. I played her. I listened and said all the right things."

I remembered how powerful I'd felt with Olivia pushed up

against the wall, the certainty I'd experienced that I could break her in half. And then she'd brushed me away effortlessly.

"Clive, the piece of shit, he spent most evenings at a bar. He was wasting the life I should've been living."

So while I was slaving away with those reports – Benny's fucking reports, most likely – he was getting sloshed. What a lovely, charming man Clive Langdale was.

"It was easy to find two escorts online who'd be up for what I was planning," Benny went on. "I explained that my friend was getting married in a month and he wanted a good time, but he didn't want them to tell him they were sex workers. He wanted to pretend it was real. He wanted cocaine too, I told them, and I'd be supplying it. They asked for more money, which was fair. This was different to their normal work. I had money saved up. I've always been a saver. I think that's one of my redeeming qualities. Or maybe it's just what happens when you grow up poor."

He stared expectantly. I worked my hand in the tape, and I forced myself to smile. "Saving money is important," I said inanely.

"I told them about the cameras. I want to make that clear. Clive was the only one recorded without his knowledge."

"He deserved it. They agreed to it."

"He comes across as so disgusting in that video. It's like those women aren't even there. It's all about him, the sweating panting pig."

I nodded in agreement, keeping my eyes fixed on his face. That seemed to disarm him somewhat, as though it allowed him to see me as a real person, or made him contemplate what he'd have to do to get rid of me.

"I followed Troy as well, Grace, I'm sorry."

"*Are* you sorry?" I asked matter-of-factly.

"Yes, no, I don't know. I was looking for any angle of attack I could find. I watched him for a few days, doing boring office stuff. I'd die if I had to work in a place like that."

"You were doing your research," I noted.

His eyes gleamed, like he suspected I was mocking him. He nodded. "I picked out his boss."

"You followed Vicky."

"It turns out she used to be an alcoholic and she goes to a support group in the city every week. I signed up for the group saying I had a drinking problem – and to be fair I was drinking more since Lacy and Boxer and Dad – and the next week, I introduced myself to her. Same routine with the fake name, two boxers' names put together."

He'd slithered behind the scenes of my life, snaking his way deeper and deeper into the fabric of me. He'd targeted my fucking *husband*, and he wanted me to smile at him, to be his best friend.

"I offered to walk her back to her car one night. She told me if I tried to kiss her she'd slam the car door on my balls. How can you not respect that sort of fire from a woman? I took it slow. I didn't want to make her suspicious."

He was telling it so calmly, so reasonably, and even as my insides warped and I felt like I was going to be sick, I kept my expression non-judgmental. *Tell me a nice long tale, Benny, so I can get my hand free.*

But what exactly could I do with a single hand?

Fuck it. I'd find out.

"I asked her about her work, waiting for her to mention Troy's name. When she did, I asked her to say it again. I'd been practicing my reaction in the mirror. I made myself look confused, then angry, then nothing, wiping it all away, like I had something to hide."

"And then what did you say?" I pushed Troy's face deep down in my gut: the way he smiled on our wedding day, still half a boy, but with a man in his eyes ready to protect our family. If I thought too much about my family, I'd melt in hopelessness.

"I told her my sister had been going out with Troy a few years ago and he'd verbally abused her and controlled her for months."

A tremor passed through me, trying to contort my features into rage. I forced my lips still.

I stared and I hated him. Troy didn't deserve any of this. He hadn't killed Hope. I had—*Benny* had.

"I said he'd cheated on you, but my sister didn't want to tear your family apart. Vicky had been cheated on in two of her three marriages. I knew this from her Facebook comments."

"You picked out her weakness."

He nodded. "But what could she do? Fire him on my word? She couldn't do anything openly. That was better as far as I was concerned. His boss would suddenly hate him and he'd have no clue why. It'd make him paranoid."

"It did make him paranoid," I said, thinking about all those arguments, all those emails, all that headache. I couldn't count the number of times Troy had ranted at me about work, about Vicky's sudden change, and here was the reason. Twisted, wrong... clever. *Evil.*

"It'd make him think about quitting his job. That was exactly what I needed."

"He'd wanted to quit for years."

"But this made it more urgent."

I coughed out a hollow laugh. "Yes, I'd say so."

"I waited."

"What for?"

"September and Russ's first year of Reception was getting closer. I knew you were nervous about it and I knew you were still looking for work."

My son's name sounded wrong coming from his mouth, like a word from a language I'd never heard before.

"The anniversary of your sister's death was timed so well. Right when I needed it to be. You were like a trapped rodent, nowhere to go, no life to live beyond your little man. Even if I used it against you, I felt bad for you."

"I'm dedicated to my son," I said, with Mother's haughtiness. "There's nothing wrong with that. I've raised him well, Benny. Don't challenge me about my son, please."

He held his hands up, like we'd bumped trolleys in the supermarket. "Sorry. I didn't mean it like that."

"No problem."

I'm awake I'm asleep I'm awake I'm asleep—

I wondered what the time was. Russ would be the most worried, shouting at Troy to find me, lying on his back and battering the floor in one of his rare temper tantrums.

"I told Clive to email you the day before Russ was due to start Reception. I didn't want to give you any time to think."

"You blackmailed Clive into giving me the job."

Benny strolled over to the stairs, bent down, and reached his hand under the step. I leaned back, cringing as he grunted and shifted around. I tugged at my wrist, but the loop was still too tight. I was perhaps halfway there, and that was being optimistic.

"Benny, please."

"Relax." He stood with a dusty pack of cigarettes in his hand. "Yeah, I blackmailed Clive. Like I said. Two birds with one stone."

49

He lit and smoked, inhaling and closing his eyes in contentment.

"Enjoying that?" I asked.

He grinned with the cigarette between his teeth. "I hid them last time I quit. I forgot they were there until just now. I know they'll kill me like they killed my old man, but goddamn, they're sweet."

"Are you going to let me go, Benny?"

"Just let me tell you what I did."

Sure, please tell me how you tortured me.

"Okay. Tell me."

"I met up with Clive after your interview."

"The interview for the fake job you'd blackmailed out of him." I was unable to keep the acid from my voice. My hands trembled with the urge to lash out at him.

"Yes," Benny said, ignoring my anger. "I told him to mention to one of his employees, one of the chattier ones, that you and him'd had a sexual relationship in the past. I wanted to play up the idea you'd screwed him to get the job. I needed you to feel

190

isolated. That was why he gave you the office too. The more alone you felt, the better."

I thought about Derrick and Zora, about their snide remarks. I'd doubted myself every step of the way, right down to thinking the confrontation with Derrick in the break room hadn't happened.

How weak was my mind, how fragile, how open to attack?

"I gave Clive things for you to do. To mess with your head. I asked him what sort of mind-fucking things a boss could do to an employee, and he looked at me all funny, trying to work out how this would hurt *him*."

I worked at the duct tape, and I thought about Mia when she was four, proudly holding a clumsy sun painting over her head. *Look, Mummy, look what I did.* I'd swept her into my arms, cradling her, terrified I'd break her if I squeezed with all the love stowed up inside of me. And this bastard wanted to take it all away.

"He gave you overtime hand-copying those reports, which is probably why he thought it was about him; he hated paying that. I went online and hired some freelancers to write the reports. I told them to include references to car crashes and hit-and-runs, but not to make it too obvious.

"Honestly, Grace, I'm surprised you didn't realise something was off with the phone call shit. Waiting for a phone to ring, getting paid for it? You're an intelligent person."

"It isn't so complicated," I said, raw, raw, *raw*. The air felt like it was attacking me. All that self-doubt, questioning the reports, thinking I was mad, for nothing. I was mad, but not in the way I'd believed. "Money is a powerful motivator."

"And everybody kept telling you it was a perfect job, a setup lots of people'd be jealous of. You were getting paid to do *nothing*."

I stared silently. He averted his gaze, focusing on his

cigarette, as though it could save him from what he'd done. I could *feel* the guilt inside of him, locked away in every gesture. It was simple for me to read; it was like looking at myself.

"I'm really impressed with you, by the way," he said. "Clive chucked you in at the deep end and you somehow didn't drown. I think he was trying to get you to quit, offering no training, no guidance. But you smashed it. Maybe your time at university helped with the reports and stuff."

"I think it must have."

I wanted to puke, to keel over and let all this tension out of me. Did he have any idea how difficult it was for me not to scream?

"You remember how you chased after me and those teenagers said they hadn't seen anyone?"

"Yes," I said, far too eager. "That was you, wasn't it? Those kids lied to me."

"Yes."

"Why the hat?" I demanded. "Both times you followed me – both times I saw you – you were wearing the same hat."

"Do you honestly not remember?" I shook my head and he sighed. "It was the hat I was wearing that evening. My old man missed it when he got rid of my clothes. I don't know why I wore it."

I knew why: to fuck with me, to torture me. But it seemed Benny Evans didn't like being confronted with his evil any more than I did.

"I paid the kids to lie to you."

"But it was so fast," I said, still doubting. There might be traps within the traps.

"It was some quick thinking on my part," he allowed. "I ran around the corner and I told the lad if you came asking for me, tell her nobody had come by and I'd give him fifty quid. They were keen and I hid in a doorway. I watched the whole thing."

I repressed a shiver. His eyes had stared from a shadowy doorway, like the eyes of a predator in the dark, a jungle cat silently appearing at the edge of a camp. But the camp was my life and he'd stalked through that instead.

Fuck Benny, and fuck anybody who wasn't called Mia or Troy or Russ.

"It was a mistake," he said. "Just like that damn phone call. I'd been drinking and I knew you were at the office. It was too tempting."

"You terrified me." I didn't have to work very hard to make my voice pitiful.

"I know." He tossed yet another butt to the floor.

This had to end soon. We'd choke to death otherwise, both of us limp and decaying in this cellar.

50

"The thing holding all of this together was the pre-workout Olivia was spiking your coffees with."

"What is pre-workout?" I asked.

"Basically it's caffeine powder. It gives you a huge jolt of energy before a workout. Some people say there's the equivalent of twenty-five coffees in one scoop. I don't know if that's true, but it's a *lot* of caffeine."

I felt the caffeine – or the lack of caffeine – setting me alight. It pumped around my body. I'd bite off the tip of my tongue for a single damn sip. It was pathetic.

"I've heard you talk about your struggle to quit, and that was three or four coffees a day. This stuff would feel like rocket fuel to you."

I laughed mirthlessly. "It did."

"The hardest part of my plan was convincing Olivia to cross that line. She's a good person. All I needed to do was get her to spike you once, because then it'd be easier. I'd hold it over her head."

I stared. He fidgeted. He cared about me, on some strange

level, even as he related all he'd done. Or was I imagining that, hoping? Perhaps he'd cut me into tiny pieces when he was done.

"I bullied her. I said some pretty unforgivable things to her. I'm not proud of the way I treated Olivia. She didn't deserve it."

"You wanted to take away my sleep. Because it would make me more likely to go insane."

"Yes," he said, reaching for another cigarette. I'd lost count of how many he'd smoked. "A day or so later, I went up to London to meet with this hacker I'd met on the Dark Web."

I snorted out a laugh, almost violent in its force. "A *hacker*?"

Benny smirked as he lit the cigarette. "I know, right? Mad times. He told me for the right price, he could do it. That was fine. I could always milk some cash from Clive. I had the video of him and those escorts. He was terrified I'd show it to his clients."

"Do what?"

Benny tapped his nose, eyes glimmering playfully. It was these moments that convinced me I was wrong. There was no humanity in Benny Evans. He was going to do terrible things to me once his tale was told.

I shifted my hand over and over, moving as subtly as I could afford.

"After that, it was time to use Olivia again. I wanted her to steal your phone for an hour." I *knew* I hadn't misplaced it. "It took more persuading and blackmail than I want to think about. 'What did this woman do to you?' she asked. I saw some real fear in her eyes. I told her you'd hurt me really bad and I wasn't ready to talk about it yet. I could tell part of her didn't believe me, but part of her *did*. Part of her *needed* to. What did it say about her if she'd trusted a monster?"

"Is that what you are, Benny?"

He flinched. "I don't know. You're looking at me like I'm one."

"That's not how I feel." I turned my eyes down. "I'm sorry if it comes across that way."

I told myself I was lying. He was a monster, and I was an innocent woman he'd mind-fucked and kidnapped and might very well kill. But every time I skipped into that corner of my mind, Hope reared up, her braid made of deformed guts, sticky with blood, and when she smiled she showed a mouthful of seashells.

Benny and Gracie, sitting in a tree, Hope sang in my mind. *M-U-R-D-E-R me...*

"The hacker came down from London. Part of me still didn't believe he could do this. But I wasn't going to back down. We went and sat in the café opposite Clive's office. We were waiting for Olivia. I'd made sure to stay round hers the night before to keep her focused. She was so torn up about it. She was having full-blown panic attacks."

"But she did it."

"Yep, and my man did some magic on the laptop. He showed me how it all worked afterward."

"How *what* worked?" I asked. "What did you do?"

"Basically, there are programs for androids that let people access their phones remotely." He waved his hands as though giving a lecture, shifting smoke around. "From their computers. I guess some tech companies and big corporations use them. This hacker had modified one of these programs so the user had complete access to the phone.

"What do you mean? I'm not the best with technology."

"It's insane, Grace, it really is," he said, ignoring my question. "Even twenty years ago this stuff would've been science fiction, but here it was, a simple double-click on my computer. It worked like a charm. *A fly on the wall.* You've heard that phrase, right? That's what it was like. I listened to you telling Troy how happy you were when he got his publication contract."

"You could *listen* to me?"

"It's incredible, isn't it? I hardly believed it at first. It was as simple as double-clicking a program on my computer."

"Jesus fucking Christ," I said, my mind throwing up a thousand moments he could've tapped in on.

He was sitting silently on the bedside table as Troy and I made love. He was perched on the edge of the kitchen counter as I scolded Russ for kicking the cupboard in beautiful boyish excitement. He was jammed into my pocket when Mia talked to me about how alone she felt.

"That was me, Grace."

"What was you?" I said, my voice shaking a little. I couldn't stop it.

"Publishers don't offer contracts to unpublished writers who haven't even finished books, not unless they're celebrities."

I let out something like a laugh and a sob, a jagged, ugly noise. If I got out of here alive, neither of us would have a job. We might lose our family home.

"I made a website and an email, and I got the advance money from Clive. I even put up some stock book covers and descriptions, and some links to Amazon and Waterstones. The links didn't go anywhere, but apparently Troy either didn't check or he didn't care."

"It meant the world to him. He's dreamed of being a writer for so, so long."

Benny refused to look at me. He skulked near the washing machine, facing the opposite wall. I stared at him, willing him to turn his gaze to mine, so he could see the hurt in my eyes, the pain he'd caused. He couldn't kill me after seeing that, could he?

"I needed Troy to quit work because then it'd make it harder for *you* to quit work, what with you being the only earner in the house."

"And then it would be easier for you to keep me in your

playground," I said. "I bet you laughed like mad when you heard me persuading Troy to quit work."

"I didn't laugh." There was a note of petulance in his voice. "I'd been thinking of a way to persuade Vicky to fire him or to somehow get him to quit. And then, shit, you'd gone and done it for me. I was relieved. But I didn't fucking *laugh*."

"You liked it though."

He kicked away from the washing machine, spinning to me. "I'm telling the damn story, not you."

I leaned back, lowering my gaze. I hated how quickly he could turn me to prey. "You're right. I'm sorry."

He paused for a time, opening and closing his lighter, *click-click-click*.

"The program came in handy the night you found Mia with all her paintings torn down," he said finally. "Remember how your phone kept interrupting you? It was Clive, right? He rang and kept hanging up. And then he sent you a text."

"But it wasn't Clive."

"I went into my program and I changed his number to mine, so when the calls and texts appeared, you'd think it was him."

I wanted to ask if he'd written those messages during my party, Hope's messages, but I knew he wouldn't like it. He needed to tell this deranged story at his own speed, apparently. He needed me to indulge him.

"Earlier that week, I'd gone to meet this bloke one of my mate's knew, one of those guys everyone's aware of. I told him I wanted as much coke as he could get me, and then I handed him what I wanted it wrapped in. It was the paper your family had for Christmas one year, posted in a photo I found on Facebook."

Underneath all the pain and rage, a flicker of relief moved through me. Here was proof, at least. I wasn't mad. I hadn't imagined it.

"When I heard how much your daughter needed you, I knew

it was my chance. Part of me didn't think you'd do it. It's really unreasonable, Grace, but by then you were starting to unravel."

"Yes." It was all I could say.

"Clive was pretty quick on his feet when he told you it was a games console. I didn't let him know I was pulling the stunt. Let the bastard be surprised. But I guess you don't get to be a successful businessman without being a good liar."

"He's a very good liar. I've witnessed it several times."

Benny paced over to me. I stiffened, sat up straighter, and prayed he didn't walk around the chair and see the mess I'd made of the duct tape. He paused just shy of me, worrying at his lighter, opening and closing it frantically. "My old man gave me this. On his deathbed, before he told me he wished I was never born, he gave me his favourite lighter. Do you think it was a sign? Do you think he wanted me to smoke myself to death too?"

"I don't know."

"No, either do I. I won't lie, Grace. Part of me liked that you were feeling like you couldn't trust yourself. That's how I've felt every day of my life after what you did to me."

51

"One day I took Hope to the fancy dress shop in town."

"So your daughter's name is Hope."

"Of course her name is Hope. It had to be. I'd stolen one Hope from the world. I owed it another."

I nodded, as though his logic made complete sense. And perhaps it did. Perhaps it was as simple as that: one optimistic, smiling girl for another.

"She loved it, running up and down the aisles, a big smile on her face."

"I took Russ to a fancy dress shop a few weeks ago," I said, remembering how he'd traipsed around the place, a pirate one minute and a space cadet the next. "He loved it too."

"I let her pick out some costumes and she chose the blue one from that cartoon, with the white wig. Ah, what's it called? There's that song, *let it goooo?* Damn, it's right on the tip of my tongue."

"*Frozen.* Mia used to love that. She claims she's outgrown it, but every now and then, she'll drop some heavy hints that she wants to watch it. She won't come out and say it though."

"She's too cool for it, eh?" Benny said, and here we were: two parents, sharing some banter, like we were friends and not torturer and victim, captor and captive.

"Yeah." I smiled, and it felt real. "She thinks she is, anyway."

I prayed I'd get a chance to watch *Frozen* with Mia again, to tease her as she resisted the urge to sing along, and then both of us would explode into song, unable to stop ourselves.

"Your little sister's hair was quite a particular shade of brown," he said. "You can see that in the photos on her memorial page and in news articles and on Facebook. My daughter's hair is blonde, like Lacy's, like yours."

"Mother called Hope's hair walnut-brown," I told him, the memory stabbing at me. I couldn't help but wonder if this was a real memory, or yet another mind-made device of torture.

"Yeah, that's it, walnut. I was hoping for one that came braided, but I could always learn how to do that. There was bound to be a tutorial on the internet."

"What did you do, Benny?" I asked, but I knew. I knew and it hurt.

"One afternoon I picked up Hope, and Grace, I have to say, I love her and I'd die before I let anything happen to her. I want to make that clear. All right?"

Emotion crept into his voice, seeming as real as his other displays. I searched his face, his furrowed brows, for any sign of artifice. Maybe he was playing me. But it felt real. It felt like he truly cared. "I believe you."

"It was all a big game to her. After a day of crazy golf, the cinema, and a burger, I took her to the offices. I knew you were working overtime. I'd paid special attention to the report you were hand-copying that evening, making sure the freelancer had added even more car collision references than usual. I told them to add some hit-and-run ones too, to really head-fuck you. I'd also bullied Olivia into giving you double doses of pre-workout, so you were properly on edge."

"I *was* on edge. It was horrible."

He flinched, as though my sentence had struck him, as though he couldn't stand being faced with what he'd done. And yet, bizarrely, he *had* to tell me. He had to make this version of himself real: the Benny who had schemed in the shadows.

"I told Hope to go into the office and look for you. She skipped ahead and the braid of her wig was bouncing on her back, the way it would if she was riding a bike. I'd bought a dress with rabbits on, like your Hope was wearing when she died, that dress, haunting my damn dreams. I bought a rock-seashell bracelet on Etsy for like three quid. It was easy."

I laughed or coughed or something. It was a noise, and it held pain and hate and humour all mashed together. Mother had always protested the bracelet was utterly unique, irreplaceable, but he'd fooled me for the price of a meal deal.

"Hope did really well. When she came skipping around the corner afterward – you were screaming – I scooped her up and cradled her to my chest and ran down the stairs. In the car, she said she'd told you her name. She thought she'd done something wrong, the poor girl. I kissed her on the head and took off the wig and told her no, she hadn't done anything wrong. She was my princess and I'd always protect her."

He wandered over to the steps, dropping down. He hugged his arms across himself and leaned back, staring at the wall. I took the chance to worry some more at the duct tape, even as my mind reeled and spun. The job, Troy's publishing deal, the present, the reports, the man in the black hat, my madness with Hope and the messages—here it was, here *he* was, the prime fucking mover.

"You sent me those messages," I said after a pause.

"I was watching you through the front-facing camera each time I typed one out." He nodded. "It was amazing, how well you managed to keep yourself together. I could see the fear in your eyes but otherwise you looked like your normal self."

"I had to. I thought I was going mad. I couldn't inflict that on my family."

"You snapped in the end though. You were finally experiencing what *I've* experienced all my damn life. You deserved it. I stand by that."

52

He sat on the step, rocking slightly, as though he was ramping up to something. But what? He'd already committed all the horror he could against me, unless he was going to end it, end *me*, and steal a mother from my children and a wife from my husband.

"In a way it's good Olivia caved and gave you my name – well, the name she thought was mine – and you came here." He stood and walked toward me. "If we weren't talking now, I don't know what my next move would be. You were stronger than I thought. Even when you were cracking up on the inside, you always managed to look like you had your shit together. You remind me of Lacy, in a way, when she's all sassy and ready to go. Capable."

"Thank you." My voice felt and sounded hollow.

"Lacy and I are getting back together," he said. "A woman like Lacy, fiery and full of life, she can't respect a worm like Clive. He isn't a man. He's not even a person. He's broken."

"You're probably right."

Benny was standing a few feet shy from me, his hands hanging at his sides, like waiting weapons that could be called to use any moment. I cringed away from him. My wrist was so close to freedom – I thought – and yet he could maul me any moment he felt like it. I was defenceless.

"When I first joined the book club, I didn't know what to expect," he mused. "I'd watched you over the years and I knew a lot about you, but I'd never talked to you. Even when I did, I didn't know if you were acting. But I know. I can tell. You care about family as much as I do."

"Of course I do," I said passionately. "Troy, Mia, Russ. They're all that matter to me, Benny, just like Hope and Lacy matter to you."

"Jesus, that club…" He grinned, shaking his head. "I've read more books since I joined than in all my school years put together."

"And you always chose books related to death. Did you want to draw out my jagged memories?"

"I don't know." He shrugged. "Maybe I was working through some stuff."

"Yeah. I'd imagine so."

"When you asked me my name, I panicked. I hadn't thought of one. Part of me assumed you'd recognise me, but the more time I spent with you, the more I thought no, she's not fucking around, she really doesn't know who I am."

"I didn't," I tell him. "I still don't remember you from that evening, not in detail. It's so hazy. Everything is such a jumble. I remember bits and pieces. I remember the top of the hill; I think I always have, in some way. But the bottom is so hard to grasp. Maybe I don't want to."

There was understanding in his eyes as he watched me, as though he felt my pain as much as I felt his. "The mind, Grace, it's a scary thing, isn't it?"

"It's the most terrifying thing there is."

"I chose Mike Tyson and George Foreman as the boxers' names I'd use for my alias," he said. "Iron Mike and Big

George Foreman. Mike Foreman. I think it has a nice ring to it."

"Sure," I agreed dully, hating that I was here, hating all he'd told me.

And yet a piece of me sang, rejoiced, cheered: I hadn't imagined it. All of it had happened. If I was mad, at least it wasn't in precisely that way.

It was hard to think of him as Mike, as the man I'd known in book club.

"Gaslighting doesn't even come close to describing what you did to me," I said.

"What's gaslighting?"

I laughed like a deranged person. *You are a deranged person.* "You're joking, right? You're the poster child for it."

"What is it?"

"It means you manipulated me to make me think I'm going insane. That's what it fucking means, and that's what you fucking did."

He shrugged. "I don't blame you for being angry."

I needed to stay calm. I was so close. I was ready to fight, to bleed, to scream. "Are you going to kill me?"

"No. I'm not a killer. I mean..."

"You didn't kill her, Benny. It was an accident."

"I ran. The *run* part of hit-and-run. That's what makes me a killer."

"You were a child. You were scared."

"You're trying to talk me into letting you go, Grace. I understand. You have a family. I'm the same. I'm not a monster. But the thing is, if I let you go, you might tell someone."

"I don't want anyone knowing about this any more than you do."

"Maybe," he allowed. "But I need some insurance."

He wandered to the bottom of the stairs and leaned down,

and then stood up with a video camera in his hand. As he flipped out the display screen, I read the words *HD* and remembered a similar camera Troy had brought home when Mia was two, beaming proudly, ready to carve our happiness into a digital forever.

"What happened the evening your little sister died, Grace?" He aimed the camera at me. "What happened at the top of that hill?"

"Do you really think I'm going to do this?"

"You don't have a choice."

53

B enny gestured with the camera. "Please don't make this harder than it needs to be."

What would my children prefer, that I died here as the mother they loved and respected, or I returned to them a killer, a broken thing, no longer the mother they knew?

"Are you just going to stare at me, Grace?"

"Please don't make me do this."

I saw Troy standing over my corpse, his face pinched tightly, his hands clenching into fists. He'd rant and rave about finding my killer and exacting vengeance. He'd charge through the morgue and roar, but in the end he'd settle down, and he'd help Mia and Russ to move on. They'd cherish my memory. They'd never know the truth.

"You have to," Benny said.

"It will tear my family to pieces."

He smiled tightly, more like a wolf flashing its teeth. "Lacy cheated on me because I was emotionally unavailable, and I *am* emotionally un-fucking-available. Because you made me kill that poor girl. My dad used his last words to tell me how much he hated me. Don't talk to me about families being torn apart."

"Benny, please—"

"No. The truth has to come out. So get on with it."

I felt my head sag, the strength trying to seep from my body. I pictured Mother in her office, surrounded by her musty paperbacks, half-living in a past she'd spent decades running away from, and all because of me, of the daughter I'd taken from her.

"I killed her." The skin on my wrist screeched in agony as the tape tore and bit. "I told her I hated her. I told her she was a baby. I told her to cycle down the hill as fast as she could, but I didn't think she would, not really."

"Yes," Benny said, sounding like a man about to devour a long-awaited meal.

"I hated her. I thought I was so cool, so much better than her. But I wasn't. I was dirt. I can never forgive myself for what I did."

Benny nodded slowly, peering at me over the top of the camera. "Good, Grace. That's good."

I heard an almost-silent ripping noise, the last of the duct tape releasing one of my hands, but the other was still secured to the chair.

Could I do this? Did I have the courage? Was I stupid enough?

I made my voice lower, lower, and kept talking about Hope, telling the truth. I loved her and I killed her.

Benny crept forward to hear the quietness of my voice.

I thought of Mia, the bundle in my arms, making me forget about university and anxiety and how much I wanted to learn about my own mind. I thought of Russ and strolling through the library in the middle of the afternoon, the rest of the world otherwise occupied, me and my son and the ancient-smelling books.

"I can do it," Troy had said, lying in bed at nineteen, before

Mia was even a dream in our minds. "I know I can be a bestseller, Grace."

"I believe in you," I'd told him.

And I had. I did.

"Grace?" Benny said.

"Ah!" I cried, swinging my body in a vicious arc.

I was almost surprised when the chair smashed into the side of his skull with a wooden *thunk*.

I ran past him like a malformed insect, loping as I dragged the chair behind me, stuck to my wrist at a jagged angle. To the bottom of the stairs. I ran. I fell. I clambered up and dragged myself toward the door.

Behind me, Benny groaned and climbed to his feet.

54

He gripped my ankle and tugged. I had my free hand around the door handle, squeezing hard, almost yanking it open before he gave me another powerful squeeze.

Benny was thin, but when I felt his hands on me I realised how deceiving his body was. The strength in his grip was almost enough to send me back-flipping down the stairs. "Wait. Fuck's sake. This is so stupid."

"Leave me alone."

I kept grabbing at the handle, trying to push it downward so the door would swing open. I was vaguely aware of the pulsing up my forearm from where the tangled chair was twisting it, from where Benny was grabbing that too, trying to bend me into submission.

I kicked blindly, felt a fleshy contact, heard a grunt.

He roared and leapt. Something bony crushed into my back, between my shoulder blades, sending me hurtling at the door and clashing woodenly with it. My jaw throbbed as I reeled and screamed.

My eyes shimmered and it was the day I'd given birth to Mia, my little bundle staring up at me with accepting eyes.

I forgive you, Mummy, I imagined her saying.

I emerged from my daze with my ears ringing and Benny's hand around my wrist, trying to guide me down the stairs the same way I might guide Russ after he'd done something silly and wonderful, like roll around in paint for the thrill of it.

"Are you done?" he snapped.

"Please let go of my hand."

He was three steps down, frowning up at me, a light bruise appearing on his cheek from where I'd swung the chair at him. The chair, perversely, still dangled from my wrist.

"You're lucky I'm so emotionally distant and cold and all the other shit Lacy calls me. Imagine what I'd do if I wasn't."

"Let go."

"We're not done here."

He tried to pull me down the stairs, but he didn't realise I could still move my other hand, the one with the chair clinging like a parasite.

He let go and tried to raise his hands when he saw what I was doing, but desperation made me quick.

With a whip-sharp motion I raked my nails down his face.

I turned for the door as he yelled and stumbled.

I pushed it open and finally the duct tape let go, the chair falling away. I ran into the house and headed for the closest exit —the back door.

It was locked.

Fuck.

I turned.

Benny was there, face bleeding, crying blood. He slinked toward me like an apex predator. "Enough games. If you try anything else, I'm gonna treat this like a boxing match. And that, Grace, means I'm gonna royally fuck you up. So just—"

I ducked my head and bull-rushed to his left, thinking, *The front door, the front door.*

Benny leapt and his wiry arm looped around my throat, compressing my airwaves.

"Are you going to make me kill you as well?" he growled in my ear.

55

"You need to stop squirming, Grace," he said, his arm across my throat. "I don't want to hurt you. Stop moving around."

"Let... me... go..."

My words came out as a smoker's wheeze.

"I will when you stop panicking."

"You said you were going to kill me." I leaned against him to release some of the pressure on my neck.

"I didn't mean it. But you have to admit you're not exactly making this easy."

"Easy? This is going to ruin me." He was loosening his grip, giving me room to speak, our bodies pressed unnaturally close together in a parody of tenderness. "It ruined you too. I understand. But that's the past; it's over. Nothing can change it. I have a family who loves me and if they found out the truth, they'd hate me."

"Do you really believe that?" I could feel the heat of his breath. "Your children love you. Your husband adores you."

"They love a woman whose beloved sister died in a tragic

accident when she was a girl. They wouldn't love the woman who talked her sister into sacrificing her life."

"What are your family like, Grace?"

I scoffed bitterly. "You *surveilled* us. You should know everything about the Dixons by now."

"Give me a reason not to ruin you. Give me a reason to care."

I blinked and tears slid down my cheeks. "There's too much." I hated the drained sound of my voice. "Mia's going to be a painter. No, she is a painter. You should see some of her work. It's incredible. My grandmother was a painter and she takes after her, my mother says, and that scares me – it terrifies me – because... well, you know why, don't you. But her art, it's beautiful, very advanced for a girl her age. She's precocious and she always has been, ever since she was Russ's age. I sometimes imagine if they were both five, what would it seem like? Mia was always so eager to be seen as older, and Russ is so wonderfully childish."

"Keep going, Grace."

"Why?" I sobbed. "Is this getting you off? Is this getting you hard, Benny? You disgusting fucking psychopath."

"Before this all started – when I first joined book club – you know, I actually wished I was a psychopath. I reckon it'd make getting revenge easier. But I'm not."

"Why do you want to hear all this? It's so messed up."

"Yeah, it's messed up."

A pause lengthened and I felt he was waiting for me to continue. My gaze moved around the hallway, over his trainers, over his daughter's pink roller skates. There was nothing to do. There was no way out. His forearm was metal across my throat.

"Troy's an amazing father," I said. "He has his hang ups, fine, especially when it comes to his career. But... you should've seen him with Mia when she was younger, the games they used to play, the worlds they used to create together. Russ likes building dens, making things, and Troy helps with that, but he doesn't like the imaginative stuff, not like Mia did. Mia and Troy would sit around for hours dreaming up fantasies. She never got tired of it, and Troy would talk so passionately about writing a series of children's books based on the worlds they invented together."

"But he didn't."

"No," I croaked. "He didn't. Please let go of my neck, Benny. You're hurting me."

He didn't let go, but he relaxed his grip a little.

"I can choke you out anytime I want. So don't try anything." I felt him thinking, the tics of his face, so close to mine, the way he was breathing, like a man pondering a problem. "This is a bit of a mess, isn't it?"

"Yes." I somehow laughed, bitter and low. "I'm..."

"You're what, Grace?"

"I'm sorry you hit Hope with your car, and that she wouldn't have been there if it wasn't for me. I'm sorry you've lived in hell since it happened, and I'm sorry for what your dad said, and that Lacy cheated on you, and that your life has been harder than it would've been without me. Okay? *I'm sorry.*"

"Thank you. That means a lot, really. But it's time to go to sleep."

"Wait, what?"

His arms tightened.

He kept me alive long enough to apologise and now he's going to kill me.

"Go to sleep, Grace."

He squeezed and squeezed and squeezed the life out of me.

56

The bed jostled up and down with the familiar motion of an excited five-year-old on a Sunday morning, the scent of bacon drifting up from downstairs and the almost undetectable sound of Mia's brushstrokes against the canvas, which I shouldn't have been able to hear, but I could. It was a beautiful sound, my daughter making art, my husband making breakfast, my son making mayhem.

"Mummy, Mummy." Russ pawed at my face. "I know you're awake."

"Nah-uh."

"You *are*. Mummy, you said we could go to the park and have bacon and have a great morning adventure, that's what you said, I remember you said that. But you're in bed and even Daddy's up and we'll have to eat the bacon before the park but that's okay. Mummy."

"Mmm," I moaned. "Five minutes."

"Promise?"

"Promise."

"But wake up, Mummy. Wake up."

"I said five minutes."

"Wake up, wake up... Grace, come on, wake up."

The bed stopped jostling up and down; Benny had finished tying my wrists in front of me with more duct tape.

My ankles were tied with rope to pipes on either side of the wall, pulled taut. My arm was throbbing and felt like it had twisted, but the pain was faraway. Everything was taking on a dreamish quality, as if I'd slipped into an upside-down land.

Benny was standing across from me. The cut on his face was long and thin, dried blood crusting around it from where I'd slashed him with my fingernails. He was just shy of my legs. My arms weren't tied to anything, only each other, so it was conceivable I could flip my body up and maybe get my hands on him, probably breaking my ankles in the process.

And then what? I'd had my best chance and I'd ruined it.

"I think my arm's broken."

He shook his head slowly. "Bruised. Sprained, maybe. If it was really broken, you'd know about it, trust me. Here." He lifted a *Frozen* plastic cup and two pills, gesturing with them. "Ibuprofen. For the pain."

I stared at the *Frozen* cup, grotesquely out of place, Elsa in her sparkling blue dress looking hopeful and self-assured as she gazed back at me.

"I hope blackcurrant's okay." He moved carefully over to me, as though afraid I'd leap at him again. "It's all I had." He read my look. "It's just ibuprofen. I promise. Plus, I'm pretty sure they've got caffeine in them. It should help."

"Fine," I said, and Benny leaned forward and helped me to gulp the pills down, leaning back cautiously as though I might lash out again.

"Now what?" he asked when I was done.

"You're asking me?" I laughed hollowly. "You're the grand conspirator."

"I wasn't recording, by the way."

"What?"

"Before, when I had the camera out and you were telling me about the evening Hope died, I wasn't recording."

"Then why..."

He scratched his face, at the shadow of a beard on his lean cheeks. "I guess I needed to hear you say it. I needed to make it real, if that makes sense? All those times at book club when you mentioned it, and all those times I overheard you at the café with Yasmin... I don't know. Shit. I told you. I started to doubt my own mind. But it's the truth, isn't it? You talked her into it."

"Yes," I said, voice raw. I'd already admitted this. How many times did he need me to say it?

Benny sunk down on his haunches, resting his forearms on his knees. "This is really tough, because I want to let you go. But let's face it. I've done a lot of illegal shit these past few months. Blackmail, extortion, I mean – goddamn – *hacking*. Not to mention assault, kidnapping. What's to stop you from going to the police?"

"I won't," I said. "I have everything to lose. My family, my parents, my life. I can't let this come out. I made our relationship into something beautiful after her death, but it was a myth, nothing more. I made it bright so I could avoid the truth. It was dark. I was a selfish teenage girl and she was my annoying little sister. I bullied her. I loved her, I know I did. Deep down. But I bullied her and it led to her death."

"But I can never be sure. If you went to the police, they might be able to go back and trace me somehow. And then it'd be my word against yours. Even if you admitted you'd talked her into riding down the hill, would they care? Are there laws for that?"

"I don't know."

"Neither do I." He bit his fingernail, dropped his hand, and rolled his neck from side to side. "I don't want to hurt you. More than I already have. As weird as it probably seems, it's meant a lot, being able to share all of this with you."

"If you let me go, I swear this ends here. We never have to see each other again. Leave me alone and I'll leave you alone."

"But the police..." He ground his teeth, looking like an animal debating a kill. "I guess there is a way, actually, a way that'll make it pretty likely you'll never tell anybody. But I'm not sure you'll like it."

"I don't care. I want to see my children again."

He nodded and rose laconically to his feet, prowling over to the staircase. He knelt down and picked up the camera. This time, he pressed a button and it made a beeping noise. A red light on the front lit up, watching.

"What really happened that evening, Grace?"

I knew he could be lying; he could knock me out and send this video to my family the second it was recorded. And yet, for some bizarre reason, I trusted him, this man who had toyed with me like I was a child's doll. Maybe it was the *Frozen* cup or the look in his eyes when he talked about his dead dog or the fact we both had children.

Or maybe I was gullible.

Maybe he was still going to kill me.

57

I sat in the passenger seat next to the man who half-killed my sister, an open bottle of vodka in my good hand. The street beyond the alleyway was dark where the lamp posts had switched off. My throat burnt with the vodka, but it took away some of the throbbing in my arm and the ache in my neck.

I looked at the clock and saw it had gone two in the morning. Troy and Mia and Russ were going to be driving themselves delirious wondering where I was.

"Don't drink too much," Benny said, as I swung back another acidic mouthful. "Just enough to seem out of it. To smell of it. You don't want to forget your story."

"I remember."

"Well, what do you remember?"

An urge: shatter the vodka bottle on the dashboard and stab the spiky edge into his throat and saw up and down until all the blood spurted out of him. But of course I wasn't going to attack him; he had the video.

"I remember," I said forcefully.

"Humour me."

"Clive fired me this afternoon and I was too ashamed to go

home. So I went to Olivia's and we had a few drinks, and a few drinks turned into a few too many. Then I wanted to sleep it off at hers. I was embarrassed to come home and admit I'd failed my family."

"And your injuries?" he asked, staring at the inky road. "Your arm. The light bruising on your neck? The redness on your cheek? That might come out as a bruise tomorrow, but it's always hard to tell. They might not even notice. But if they do?"

"I fell when I was drunk."

Benny nodded. "I'll sort it with Clive and Olivia. If anybody asks them, which I doubt they will, but if they do... their stories'll match, all right?"

"How helpful. Are we becoming best friends, Benjamin?"

"My mum used to call me Benjamin."

"Do you miss her?"

He shrugged. "Not as much as I used to."

"I hate you," I said, the confession surprising me more than it bothered him.

"I wouldn't expect any different. Not after today. Not after everything I've done."

I found myself laughing, ironic and sharp at first, but then the vodka and the bizarreness of this moment warped it into something else, a choking yelp. I turned away and caught myself in the reflection of the window. I noticed the lines around my eyes and the sagging of my cheeks. *Hope should be here. Not me.*

"You're the only one who can ever know the truth. The man who tortured me. For the rest of my life, you'll know more than my husband, my children, my best friend. My parents."

"You won't tell anybody?"

"Of course not." I imagined their faces flooding with pain and resentment. *We loved you before you told us.* "I think I've made that clear."

"I thought you might, not all of it. But what happened with you and Hope. I'm sorry."

"I find it hard to believe you're capable of being sorry. Considering everything you did, all the effort you went through... why would you be sorry now when you weren't before?" I was sitting up, clutching the vodka bottle so hard the glass was digging into my palm. "Did telling me your story miraculously make you human again?"

His eyes widened and tragic pain touched his features, and then he hid it all with a smirk. "You're one poetic lady, Grace, I'll give you that. *Miraculously make me human again*. You know what, you might be right. I guess you don't know how crazy something is until you say it out loud."

"No." I swigged the vodka, let it singe the inside of my throat. "I guess you don't."

He took the bottle and swigged, and then his lips twisted and he coughed. "That's fucking horrible."

A smile shaped my lips without my say-so, a drunken manoeuvre, or perhaps that was another excuse; perhaps I needed to stop making excuses. Perhaps Benny had made me smile and that was the end of it, this man I should hate – *did* hate – and who knew me better than Troy ever could. Because he understood I was evil as well as good, if I was good at all.

"Don't use the video. Please."

"I won't," he said. "It's—"

"Insurance."

"Exactly."

The headlights from my taxi cut across the night and, on the dashboard, my phone vibrated. The screen lit up. Again. Troy and Mother and Father had been ringing ever since Benny returned my phone.

I'll have to get a new phone, I thought disjointedly.

"I wish I could say it's been a pleasure," I said. "But, really, it's been the exact opposite. I assume you're done with the book club now?"

"Would you like me to be?"

I don't know.

"Of course I would. It would be rather awkward now, wouldn't it? In fact, if I don't see you until we're both burning and rotting in hell, it will be far, far too soon. Do we understand each other?"

"Sure. No problem."

I was about to climb from the car when a thought occurred to me.

"What is it, Grace?" Benny said, reading me. He'd had enough bloody practice.

"It's silly, but my car's at your house."

"Give me the keys. It'll be waiting for you tomorrow morning." He looked closely at me, sensing my natural aversion to the idea. "I'm not going to steal your car, Grace."

"No, you'd never do such an evil thing," I said, voice tinged with irony.

He shrugged, waited. I took my keys from my handbag – which he'd returned to me with my phone – and placed them on the dashboard. "You're going to have a busy night."

"It's okay." He smiled, seeming once again like cocky book-club Mike. "I don't sleep much."

I laughed, an unnatural sound, hating myself for it, hating *him*. I killed the noise. "Fuck you, Benny."

"Fair enough. One more thing, and then I'll let you go."

A deathly tingle crept up my spine. This was the moment his face would warp, the monster would emerge, all teeth and sarcasm. *Did you really think I'd let you go, you stupid fucking whore?* He'd flick a knife from his sleeve and slice at my face, or maybe... yes, maybe the taxi wasn't a taxi, but one of his friends coming to cause me more harm. Maybe this was all a big joke. I tried to tell myself I was being paranoid, but that was difficult when the paranoia of these past couple of months had been proven right.

I turned.

He was holding a small black rectangle. I looked closer, aided by the light of my rioting phone, and saw it was a USB memory stick.

"What is it?"

"Insurance."

My hand closed around it and, briefly, our fingertips touched.

I broke the contact and climbed from the car, leaving the vodka, walking in my work clothes toward the taxi, heels clicking, just another drunk woman on her way home.

58

"Mum? What's wrong? Mum?"

Mia had never sounded younger as she stood at the door, still in her school uniform. I leapt forward, forgetting the pain in my arms as I wrapped them around her and pulled her close, crying into her hair. Mia's hands slowly rose and she held on to my back. "It's okay, Mum."

"Where's Russ?" I sobbed.

"He's in bed," Troy said, peering at me from the dimly-lit hallway, the light coming from the living room where I could hear voices raised.

Mother. Father.

What were they doing here? They couldn't possibly be concerned about the woman who'd killed their favourite daughter.

Troy was wearing a faded comic-book T-shirt and baggy jogging bottoms, but as he stepped forward he looked official, like he should be in a policeman's uniform. "Where have you been, Grace? We've all been worried sick. Jesus, you can't just disappear. What happened?"

226

"Yeah, Mum," Mia said, a tremble in her voice. "Why are you crying?"

"I love you." I kissed her forehead.

"I love you too. But what's wrong? Please tell me what's wrong."

"I lost my job," I croaked, and then Mother appeared behind Troy, wearing a stiff off-white blazer and chinos, her heeled boots matching the dull silver of her earrings, her hair piled artfully atop her head and her sharp judgemental nose aimed at me.

I thought of her as an unseen girl in a giant crumbling house, peering through an old door as her mother dangled there, throat slit, and I thought of her muffling her sobs in a pillow for years after Hope died, and how she'd never looked at me – never seen me – since then, because she'd chosen not to. I thought about what would happen if I told her the truth: told all of them the truth. I knew I never would.

"Mum." I walked toward her on shaky legs. "I'm so sorry. I lost my job, Mum."

My voice sounded pathetic even to my own ears, a fully-grown woman begging for her mother, but unbelievably Isabella Addington came forward and looped her arm around me.

"Come on. I do believe you've had too much to drink."

She sat me down in the living room. Father placed his hand in mine and gave it a squeeze. Troy sat opposite and frowned at me, his eyes already calculating. What did my job loss mean for us? What did it mean for his writing career?

You know exactly what it means for his writing career.

"What happened, sweetheart?" Father asked.

"I failed you." Another wave of tears crushed into me, as though the full magnitude of what I'd done could only be real with the reflected pity in my family's eyes.

Mother kept stroking my back and whispering in my ear, telling me I'd failed nobody. I couldn't stop crying. Her kindness was killing me. My ice-queen mother had my hand in hers and she was telling me she'd protect me. For the first time in almost two decades she was telling me it was all going to be okay.

"Where are the children?" I asked when I could finally speak again. I had no clue how long I'd sat there, sobbing, but Mia was gone.

"In bed," Troy said. "I told you I was taking her up so we could talk."

"I know," I lied. "I remember."

I remember, ha-ha-ha.

I reached for the coffee somebody had brought me. It was in my World's Greatest Mum mug, the one Mia and Russ had gifted me last Mother's Day. The sight of it almost made me choke on sobs again. I pushed them down and sipped. And then, finding it was lukewarm, I downed the entire mug. "Are the children okay?"

"They're fine," Troy said. "A little shaken up. A little worried. I'm worried too. We all are."

"Of course. You have every right to be. What I did, it was wrong. It was unacceptable. Unforgivable." They thought I was talking about staying out late and getting drunk, about causing them a few hours of concern. They didn't know I was talking about Hope and rain and death. "I'm not a good person."

"Grace, you're the best person I know." Troy strode across the room and knelt down, like when he'd proposed, kneeling down in our flat when I was four months pregnant, saying some nice words, no rigmarole, and yet it was still achingly romantic. "You're an incredible mother. I've been so proud of you these past few months. Losing your job doesn't change that. Tell us what happened."

I told them about Clive firing me. I was still within my

probation period so he didn't need to give me notice. I told them how I'd gone over to Olivia's and we'd gotten absolutely sozzled because that's what people did when they lost their jobs. I told them about the shame I felt, and how I'd kept my phone off out of humiliation.

Lies, lies, but part of me believed them, because I was practiced at tricking myself. I'd spent years purposefully ignoring a truth that would've cracked me in half had I looked at it.

"I'm sorry. I know it was wrong."

Mother, to my utter disbelief, tutted and said, "Wrong? Grace, you've been under an awful lot of pressure and of course this is a difficult time for you. Now, yes, you're correct. It was silly of you not to contact any of us. But punishing yourself isn't going to help."

I looked into her eyes. I imagined the way she must've smiled when she first cradled Hope in her arms, gazing down at her in wonder. They'd thought she couldn't have any more children. Hope was a miracle. And I'd taken her.

"I love you so much, Mum. You know that, don't you?"

She flinched. Her eyes flitted as though looking for an escape. Something in me dropped. But then she said, "Of course I know, dear. I love you too."

I could only marvel at the way she was behaving, but this was the most emotional I'd been with her after Hope's death. I'd never cried in front of her, asked for her help, shared my feelings, and here it was, spilling out. Pathetically, yes, but it was there all the same. Maybe it meant something to her. Maybe she really did care.

Soon Troy was helping me to bed. He laid me down like I was a child and then left to say goodbye to my parents. I turned on the lamp and reached across to the bedside table, rooting around for the photo of Hope, the one of her sitting on her brand-new bike, taken a few days before her death.

She was gleaming and very much alive, one foot on the pedal like she was ready to speed off and make her mark on the world.

I held it to my chest and closed my eyes.

59

I woke to the smell of coffee and a throbbing that went all through my body, from the tips of my toes up to my scalp. I blinked and felt the stickiness of my eyes and the hung-over dryness of my tongue. With some effort, I sat up.

Troy sat on the edge of the bed, his hair ruffled and his eyes pensive. "Morning. Well, afternoon."

"What time is it? Where are the children?"

"They're at school. I thought I'd let you sleep."

"Thanks." I brought the coffee to my mouth and sipped, craving the caffeine, my body a mutiny of impulses after so many weeks hooked on Benny's shit. "What time is it?"

"Half one." He ran a hand through his hair. "I'm sorry, Grace. I'm so sorry."

"For what?"

"I knew you were having a tough time at work. Not how bad, obviously. But I knew you were stressed out. I was selfish. I ignored it because I wanted to live my stupid fucking dream of being this big-time writer. I need to face reality. That's never going to happen."

"It is," I told him, placing the coffee down and moving closer, reaching out and clasping his sweaty hand. I was stunned when he didn't pull away in disgust. *Killer*. "You're talented, Troy. I believe in you."

"I lost the writing contract."

"Oh."

"Oh?" He tilted his head. "Is that all you've got to say? It's a pretty big blow, especially after you lost your job."

"I know. But we'll get through it together."

"They emailed me out of the blue and said they were no longer interested," he said as dusty sunlight settled on his grim-set face. "They loved my stuff. I'm a talented writer. But they're not interested. How does any of that make sense?"

"It doesn't. It seems like these things rarely do."

"So what the hell are we going to do now? We've got bills. We've got the mortgage. My car isn't even paid off."

"Troy, look at me."

He dragged his gaze to mine. Time flitted and we were at the student's union again. He was a passion-filled young man with sharp eyes and sharp ambitions and we made a silent promise to take each other as high as we could possibly go, together, always together. And then I saw my husband, this mature man, this realistic man even if he sometimes lived in make-believe worlds. A tsunami of love crashed down on me.

"Do you love me?"

He laughed, as if the question was absurd. "Of course I do."

"And I love you. And I love Russ and Mia and I think you might too."

"Yes, Grace," he said ironically. "I love my children."

"Don't you see, then?" I leapt at him, landing in his lap in a tangle of limbs. "Everything's going to be okay. Love will..."

"Set us free?" he teased.

"Maybe. As silly as it sounds, yes, maybe it will."

"I hope love can pay the bloody mortgage too."

"We'll be okay. I know we will."

"In the meantime I need to get down to the library. Our printer's decided to pack it in and I've got to print some CVs."

"*Print* some CVs? What on earth for?"

"Some people prefer hard copies, believe it or not. Maybe I'll get a job for that mysterious client of yours. Did you ever find out who he was?"

"No," I said; I lied.

"Ah, well. None of those bastards deserve you anyway. Do you want anything while I'm out?"

"I'm fine, thank you. Just maybe a kiss?"

He smirked, looking fifteen years younger, and then leaned down and brushed his lips against mine. "Good enough?"

I grabbed him and ran my hands through his hair, and kissed him hard. He made an animal noise and we sank deeper into the kissing. When we fell apart he gave me a look that said, *Later?* I puckered my lips, feeling suddenly and inexplicably sexy, despite the vodka breath and the soreness and the pain whirring through me.

He left the room and I returned to my coffee. When I heard the front door close, I grabbed the USB stick Benny had given me. It was still in my pocket. I'd slept in my clothes.

I grabbed Troy's laptop and logged on and inserted the memory stick.

There it was: a video file.

I double-clicked and immediately the room filled with piggish grunting, Clive's voice, and there were the two women, completely naked and young-looking. Clive was snorting coke off this one's arched back while he toyed idly with the other one's privates.

"Whore," he growled hatefully, rubbing the powder from his

nose. "Dirty bitch. You're both a couple of fucking sluts, aren't you? Aren't you? *Say it.*"

I shut the laptop and took out the USB stick, and then got out of bed and walked into the en suite.

It was time to go to work.

60

The pulsating in my arm was becoming quite persistent, a pain I'd soon have to address. Perhaps I could feign an accident or discreetly take a visit to the doctor's, but for now I was content to let it niggle at me, an ignored repressed thing, which I was good at: ignoring, repressing. My face had only reddened slightly and the mark was easily concealed with make-up.

Benny had delivered my car, as promised. It was unlocked and the keys were inside. I tried not to think of him gliding silently through the night, past our house. It made me want to laugh and cry at the same time.

I drove into the city, to the waterfront, stopping outside the office and staring up at the redbrick façade. How excited and hopeful I'd been a couple of months ago, gazing at this building like it was a desert oasis. The thought of stepping inside sickened me.

My mobile rang. I pulled it out – the screen was cracked from last night – and Mother's name blinked jaggedly on the display. I thought about not answering, knowing Benny could be listening. But it didn't matter. He'd heard enough already. Soon I'd stamp this phone into tiny fragments.

I swiped over crumbly glass.

"Good morning, Grace. I wanted to check everything was all right."

Not even close. "Yes, thank you. I feel much better this morning."

"That's good. You were in such a dreadful state last night and, well, I was wondering if you mightn't like to pop round for a piece of cake this afternoon? You can bring the children, of course."

"I'd love to." And then, before my nerve could fail me, I blurted, "Mum."

I felt her flinch at the use of the word *Mum*, but she didn't correct me. "Very well, then. I'll see you soon."

"I love you." I hung up quickly, not waiting to hear if she'd say it back.

I climbed from the car and gripped the USB stick firmly.

Olivia's face turned ghost-white when she saw me striding across the Pen, approaching her desk.

"Uh, Grace." She gripped the edge of the desk like she was debating hiding beneath it. "I didn't think you'd be in today."

I bared my teeth like a predator. Like Mike, like Benny. "I was absolutely dying for one of your gorgeous coffees. I know it's awfully rude, Olivia, me barging in like this, an ex-employee – a woman who fucked Clive to get the job, no less – but I've been unable to sleep thinking about Olivia Melhuish's infamous coffee concoctions."

She stared at me in abject horror. "Grace..."

"Is Clive in?"

"He's in a meeting, actually."

"I'll go right through, shall I?"

I felt a note of satisfaction at the way she slumped down,

powerless as I strode toward Clive's office. And then something else, a knifing guilt. *She was a pawn. She's not to blame.*

I ignored the frantic thumping of my heartbeat and pushed the door open. Clive was aiming his salesman's grin at a client. I could only see the back of his head, but I recognised the grey-haired man as Timothy Richardson, the man whom Clive and I had been fleecing for months.

Clive's expression faltered when he saw me, his surface charm draining away. "Grace. I'm a little busy at the moment."

I revealed the USB stick with a magician's flourish. "Shall I wait outside?"

"No!" he blurted, causing Timothy to tense up. "No, of course not. We can sort this out. Yes. Fine. Great. Tim, if you'll give me a moment."

"Um, sure. I'll be outside."

I passed him on my way in, muttering, "You can do better than Clive, Mr Richardson."

He flinched and left, and I shut the door behind him, turning to Clive.

"What do you want?" he asked. "Has Benny sent you to stir up more trouble? You and him have been working together since day fucking one, haven't you?"

I smiled and shrugged. *Clive, if only it was that simple.*

"Let's start with what I don't want."

"Fine. And what's that?"

"I don't want to ruin your business. I don't want to cause any harm to your employees, even though a lot of them, frankly, are utter fucking arseholes."

"How do I know that thing is what you're implying it is?" He took a bottle of whisky from a desk drawer and poured himself a glass. *The prick thinks he's in* Mad Men. "You could be bluffing."

"Check your email."

He clenched his teeth and turned on his computer.

A minute later he turned back to me and his eyelids seemed heavier. He necked the whisky, poured another glass, necked it, and poured another. I was sitting opposite him, idly studying my fingernails. "What *do* you want then?"

"First of all I want you to know you're a disgusting fucking pig for the way you treat the girls in this video. You look pathetic, old, worn out. You look sad, Clive, so very sad."

"Okay." He didn't care what I thought, only what his clients thought. It was classic Clive. "But what do you *want*, Grace?"

"A fair severance package."

"Define fair."

"Six months' pay in a lump sum."

"You're joking."

"Do you want me to release the video?"

What a grimy situation this was. Benny had a video of me and so my hands were tied; I had one of Clive and it was the same for him. We were all down in the muck and I hated it. But there had to be something good that came of this, some small sign it wasn't all soundless noise.

"It looks like I don't have a choice," he said. "You know, I actually liked you. You were damn good at this job."

I stood up, telling myself the compliment didn't mean anything. I wasn't proud. "I'm sure you'll make this a priority."

I walked from the office, returning to the Pen.

It all seemed drabber, somehow. The carpet seemed grimier, the lights more artificially stark. I thought about Mia and Russ and the vividness of the living room when his toys and her paints and pencils were scattered everywhere.

I hate this place, I thought, and I left.

~

I sat in Queen's Square, just as I did when I'd first interviewed for this job, but now an eerie calm fell over me. The Pandora's Box in my mind was cracked open. I felt it inching more and more ajar each second, and I knew one day the lid would fly off completely. I'd remember it all in high-definition detail instead of hazily, intermittently. Would I be able to face it? I didn't know. But I had to try.

My phone pinged with a bank alert. Clive had transferred the funds.

I thought about the bottom of the hill and the ruined bike – the wheel wasn't spinning, of course it wasn't – and I saw Benny in his black hat. I saw, in a passing vignette, a broken girl lifeless in the rain.

I opened my internet browser and navigated to the hit-and-run charity. I added every last penny to the donations field.

And then I stopped. I stared at the figure.

What the fuck was I doing?

Hope was my past. What I'd done to her was wrong, evil, unforgivable.

But Mia, Troy, Russ: they were my future. They needed my help, especially with both our incomes gone.

I changed the figure, giving a third of it to the charity. It wouldn't do much to ease my conscience – I sensed only time could do that, and even that might fail – but it was something, a gesture to the universe. It was fucking *something*. It had to be.

There was a Comments field. I typed in one word. I stared and wondered if this could lead anybody back to me.

I clicked Submit.

Hope, I'd typed.

Just *Hope*.

61

I sat in my car, looking across the sun-dappled street at Benny's house.

It had been two days since I'd donated to the hit-and-run charity, and a theory had taken root in my mind, niggling no matter how much I tried to ignore it. As I talked to Troy about possible job opportunities, about how I was still determined to get part-time work – as I played with Russ and chatted with Mia – as I white-knuckled my insanity, ate cake and drank coffee with Mother, *Mum*, through everything, it was there.

It made sense.

Benny was a liar. Of course he was capable of buying a few props that would make it seem like he had a daughter. It would add validation to his sob story. Pink roller skates in the hallway, a bike in the garden, a *Frozen* mug, all things that could've been for show.

I had to know his story was true. Because otherwise nothing meant a damn thing. There was something else too, a savage inner voice telling me I was obligated to get revenge.

Steal the confession, hand him over to the police. *And then he'll tell everybody what you really did*. But without the confession, nobody would believe him.

The door opened and a little girl came out, wearing full protective padding and a pink helmet, walking awkwardly in the roller skates. She walked up the path and into the residential road, Benny following after her.

I found myself wanting to shout at them across the street. Benny should've known better than to let a child play in the road.

But there was no traffic and Benny stood close to her the whole time, his eyes scanning up and down the street and then settling on me. He stared and I stared back, unsure of what to do. Then he said something to his daughter and they both started toward the car.

I snatched my hand to the ignition, instinct telling me to flee. But too soon they were there, standing a few feet away, Benny raising his hand in a friendly-seeming way. He had stitches on his cheek from where I'd gouged him with my nails. Unfairly, I wanted to tell him I was sorry; a discreet visit to the doctor had told me that my injuries were superficial, and would heal with time.

The girl's blonde hair spilled from her helmet, her face nothing like my Hope's. I was stunned I'd gotten them confused. Darkness and madness and paranoia will do that to a person.

"Hey, Grace." Benny smiled when I rolled down the window a few inches. He seemed like a different man, Mr Family. "I was just telling Hope you're not angry with her for the prank at your office. She's feeling a little guilty."

"I didn't mean to scare you," the girl said shyly, looking at her dad even as she spoke to me.

"It's okay." My feelings were suddenly muted. "It was all a big game."

"See?" Benny reached down and squeezed her shoulder. "You didn't do anything wrong, sweetheart."

"Can I go skate, Daddy?"

"Yeah, course. Stay on the pavement until I'm done talking with my friend."

She nodded and skated clumsily away, Benny watching the road until she was safely on the pavement. He turned to me, looking more surprised than angry. "It's weird, Grace, this doesn't look like hell."

"What?"

"You said you only wanted to see me again in—"

"Yes, I remember," I snapped, thoughts fuzzy with caffeine withdrawal. I was still drinking coffee, but nothing as strong as the drugs with which he'd dosed me. "I wanted to..."

His eyes gleamed perceptively. "To make sure I didn't invent my daughter and my girlfriend."

"Exactly."

"Well, she's there, she's real. Anything else?"

Thoughts of revenge drained away at the sight of his Hope skating up and down the path, lost in the activity, the same way my Hope looked as she ran across the beach or the stones, searching, always searching.

In the front window Lacy stood with her arms folded, watching us. She was wearing an apron with little figures on. I was too far away to tell what they were, but I imagined rabbits, dozens of them, dotted all over the apron. Soon she'd turn away and lift some home-cooked dish from the oven, steam wafting around her.

They were a family – a little broken, a little lacking, a little wonderful – just like mine, and it hurt, and it mattered. I didn't know quite what to make of it.

The girl turned at the end of the path, making a tight pirouette, opening her mouth in a proud giggle at the move.

"Grace?" Benny prompted.

I cleared my throat. *Bleed. Kill yourself. Go insane. Die.* "Take care of your family."

"I will. And you take care of yourself. I mean that."

I didn't reply; I didn't know what to say.

I backed the car out and drove slowly down the street. The girl watched me go, lifting her hand in a wave. She was so adorable, so full of life. I couldn't stop myself from smiling and waving back.

62

"I get to be the doggy," Russ said, reaching for the silver Monopoly piece.

We were sitting in the living room around the board, the night cold and dark and easy to forget beyond the glass. The room was warm, the central heating blasting and making my cheeks glow red. I shared a look with Troy, a half-happy look. We knew this moment was special, and we knew how hard we needed to fight for it.

With his *advance*, our savings, my final pay cheque, and the money I'd kept from Clive's blackmail, we had some breathing room. And after?

We'd work at it together. As long as they still loved me; as long as they never knew the truth.

I was the hat. Mia was the boot and Troy was the battleship.

Russ walked his dog across the board, grinning as he made barking sounds. Fear quivered in me when I thought about Troy returning to work. What if the progress Russ had made at Reception was all for naught? But Russ was starting to adjust. Things were getting better and we'd make sure it stayed that way.

We rolled and Mia got the highest score, and then she rolled for her turn.

"Great." She moved her boot to Park Lane. "I'll buy it."

"No, you gotta go round first," Russ said.

"It's not in the rules." Mia sighed. "Dad, tell him that's not in the rules."

"Afraid not, little man. She can either buy or start a bidding war."

"When we play at *Ryan's* house, we go round."

Russ and Ryan, a new friend, just like he'd wanted when this all started. Perhaps they'd stay friends through all of primary school, maybe even secondary. Perhaps my son would be okay. Perhaps we all would.

"Well, Ryan doesn't know how to play," Mia scoffed. "I'm buying it. Dad, can you do my money please?"

They made the exchange and Russ sulked, but by the time it was his turn his mood had passed. Mia reached across and ruffled his hair. Troy and I shared a smile.

I wanted to capture this moment. I wanted to glue it into my memory.

I wanted the concept of my memory to be a true, solid thing, something I could rely upon and never had to second-guess, because I wasn't sure anymore. I wasn't certain I could count on this moment in the future; it might take on a different pallor, paint fading in the sun.

I wanted to cling on to every single second so I could always be the person I was now: the wife, the mother who made her children smile and laugh.

Not *the killer*. Not *the liar*.

All too soon this evening would pass, reshaping and dying, and something new would take its place. Maybe I'd be the real me in my recollections. Or maybe I'd become the person I wished I was, or the person I never wanted to be. Most likely, I knew, I would be something in between.

"Mummy," Russ said, calling me from my reverie.

I looked up. "Yes?"

He was smiling, holding out the dice. "It's your turn."

THE END

ACKNOWLEDGEMENTS

If I tried to list every single person I owe thanks to – who contributed to this novel's existence in even minor ways – I'd add at least one hundred pages to this book's length. Which is to say if I miss anybody, I am very, very sorry.

I have so much gratitude for my editor, Morgen Bailey. Working with her was an absolute pleasure and she made my little story so much better. (Why didn't I think of removing the duct tape?!) It is impossible to overstate how grateful I am to her. She did exceptional work and read the novel front to back several times, until she must've been absolutely sick of it.

Everybody at Bloodhound Books has been professional, welcoming, and all around amazing to work with. Betsy and Fred, the wonderful cover designers, my proofreader, Shirley, the super-conscientious Tara, social-media guru Maria... all of you have my deepest thanks.

This has been a crazy journey and I've already made some friends for life. I can't list them all, but Keri Beevis, Patricia Dixon and Heather Fitt deserve a special mention. Trish, you were the one who welcomed me with open arms into this bookish world, you were there for me when I was feeling low.

You will never know how grateful I am. The laughs the four of us have shared have been the highlight of my publication journey. (That will change the second I get a film deal, but there ya go.)

I thank my dad, Raymond, for being the silent hero people rarely write books about. I thank my mum, Betsy, for inspiring much of what happens in this book, and for making me a bacon sandwich on Christmas Eve. I thank my brothers, Ben and Jake, for playing PlayStation VR with me and generally being the best. I thank my English teacher, Rachael Hobson... Miss, if you're out there, I made it! I thank my dogs, Loki and Gizmo, for being cute and unmanageable and perfect. I thank my friends, James and Marshall and Kane and Joey, for making me laugh and letting me go a little crazy every now and then.

Lastly, most importantly, I thank my wife. Krystle, without you I never could've written a single page, let alone a whole book. You inspire me more and more every day.

(PS. If you have got this far, it means you have found something in my writing compelling enough to keep you going... in that case, I very humbly and not at all presumptively thank you for leaving a review on Amazon, and I thank you for telling your friends about my book, and for heading over to Facebook and joining the Paperback Writers group where we hold competitions and get up to all sorts of bookish shenanigans.)

A NOTE FROM THE PUBLISHER

Thank you for reading this book. If you enjoyed it please do consider leaving a review on Amazon to help others find it too.

We hate typos. All of our books have been rigorously edited and proofread, but sometimes mistakes do slip through. If you have spotted a typo, please do let us know and we can get it amended within hours.

info@bloodhoundbooks.com

Printed in Great Britain
by Amazon